THE NARRATIVE POEMS

WILLIAM SHAKESPEARE

THE NARRATIVE
POEMS

AND POEMS OF DOUBTFUL

AUTHENTICITY

EDITED BY RICHARD WILBUR AND

ALFRED HARBAGE

PENGUIN BOOKS

Penguin Books Ltd, Harmondsworth,
Middlesex, England
Penguin Books, 625 Madison Avenue,
New York, New York 10022, U.S.A.
Penguin Books Australia Ltd, Ringwood,
Victoria, Australia
Penguin Books Canada Limited, 2801 John Street,
Markham, Ontario, Canada L3R 1B4
Penguin Books (N.Z.) Ltd, 182–190 Wairau Road,
Auckland 10, New Zealand

First published in *The Pelican Shakespeare* 1966
This revised edition first published 1974
Reprinted 1979, 1982

Library of Congress catalog card number: 75-98380

Printed in the United States of America by
Kingsport Press, Inc., Kingsport, Tennessee
Set in Monophoto Ehrhardt

CONTENTS

THE NARRATIVE POEMS

INTRODUCTION

And Shakespeare, thou whose honey-flowing vein,
Pleasing the world, thy praises doth obtain;
Whose *Venus* and whose *Lucrece*, sweet and chaste,
Thy name in fame's immortal book have placed:
    Live ever you, at least in fame live ever;
    Well may the body die, but fame dies never.
Richard Barnfield, 1598

Some poetic genera have survived in our practise, understanding, or both, and some have not. The sonnet, and even the sonnet-sequence, are still being written, and the earliest English sonnets (Shakespeare's among them) are still being read. We have, in consequence, a going sense of what the sonnet can accomplish, and also of what subjects and attitudes traditionally belong to it. But of the masque, for instance, we have no corresponding natural awareness; only the specialist in Stuart literature could say whether Robert Frost's *A Masque of Reason* is in any way a revival of the art-form, and most readers have enjoyed Milton's *Comus* without much notion of its relation to the norms of courtly entertainment. We can, of course, find an antique work good without knowing precisely how it is "good of its kind"; but much depends, in such cases, on the simplicity of the convention and on the persistence of analogous forms of poetry. The two long poems which, in Barnfield's judgment, were to assure Shakespeare's immortality are complex and confusing in relation to a number of conventions, literary and pictorial, and those conventions are dead; poems of the kind are no longer written, and few of them are still read. Since one cannot cheer without knowing what the game is, the reader of these poems today is likely to find himself wishing for some historical guidance.

The literature on the poems is extensive, but that vast machinery of mediation does not answer one's questions with the sure brevity of a computer. Some things are clear, however. The *Venus*, of which I shall speak first and most, is an Ovidian narrative poem which derives the greater part of its material from passages of the *Metamorphoses*: those on Venus and Adonis, on Narcissus, and on Salmacis and Hermaphroditus. The epigraph, moreover, is taken from Ovid's *Amores*. Shakespeare was thus promising in some measure to emulate a witty, charming, and delicately sensual Latin poet. He was also choosing to retell a tale which every literate person knew in the original, and which had already been variously treated by English poets: by Golding in his moralized translation of Ovid, by Spenser, by Lodge, and by several others.

The dedicatee of Shakespeare's poem was the Earl of Southampton, a young courtier who employed John Florio as his tutor in Italian and was presumably a sophisticate. Given such a first reader, Shakespeare would doubtless be inclined to make his poem not a moral allegory (as medieval Ovidian tradition would have urged) but lightly erotic and fashionably artificial, in the manner of Marlowe's *Hero and Leander*. If these were Shakespeare's desiderata, he cannot be said to have consistently achieved them; but that he aimed well enough at the tastes of Southampton and his like is indicated both by Gabriel Harvey's reference to *Venus*' rage among the "younger sort" and by the greater assurance of Shakespeare's dedication of *Lucrece* to Southampton one year later.

The poem has been praised for its quick, decisive beginning, and it is true that the first stanza provides the time, some sense of place, the persons, their motives, and the beginning of the action: Adonis is off to hunt, and the enamored Venus comes running to intercept him. But this sort of narrative urgency does not continue; indeed, it stops right there, and we see at once that Shakespeare is not plunging into his narrative but getting some part of it over with. As Venus begins her leisured and mannered importunities in stanza 2, it is clear that her much-told story will not be told here for story's sake. There is no question, of course, of any incapacity for narrative writing, as one may tell by this later stanza in which Venus, seeking Adonis, encounters his wounded and complaining hounds:

> When he hath ceased his ill-resounding noise,
> Another flap-mouthed mourner, black and grim,
> Against the welkin volleys out his voice.
> Another and another answer him,
>> Clapping their proud tails to the ground below,
>> Shaking their scratched ears, bleeding as they go.
>>>> (919 ff.)

That is cleanly written, it is vivid for eye and ear, and it does not hover too much, but keeps the story in motion; the pack goes bleeding by, and Venus moves on with increased anxiety toward the discovery of Adonis. But when she does find him, when she "unfortunately spies / The foul boar's conquest on her fair delight," the event is almost parenthetical, and the poem characteristically swerves from direct narrative into a cascade of similes, in which Venus' afflicted eyes are likened to fading stars, retracting snail-horns, and the unnerved intelligence-officers of a court.

Not only are the few happenings of the plot minimized in favor of such embroidery, but no depth or intelligible development can be found in the characters or relationship of Venus and Adonis. Adonis is a boy who likes hunting and is prodigiously insusceptible to love; sullenly, and on the whole mutely, he resists Venus' pleas and caresses from beginning to end. The one other thing we know about this rudimentary person is that he does have the decency to resuscitate a woman who has fainted. Venus, for her part, is at one moment moved by pity, but everything else she does and says – her wrestlings, her sophistries, her tricks, her reproaches – is traceable to her one allotted motive: a sometimes etherealized sensual passion. The death of Adonis saddens but does not chasten her, and though we leave her "immured" in Paphos she has not conceivably become a conventual type.

The poem differs from Ovidian poetry generally in containing a very high proportion of dialogue, but its many speeches do not serve, by characteristic cadence and lexicon, or by the betrayal of emotional pattern or conflict, to give the speakers any individual savor, or psychic volume. Their attitudes have been assigned in stanza 1, and whenever they sound unlike themselves we are dealing not with the emergence or revelation of a new quality but with inconsistency on the part of the author. For example, in her prophecy that sorrow shall hereafter attend on love (1135 ff.) Venus takes high moral ground and deplores jealousy, deceit, and unrestraint in a manner which is foreign to her but convenient for the poet's local purposes. Adonis asserts (409 ff.) that he knows not love and does not care to know it, but in the next stanza argues from a quite different and more knowing position that one may be spoilt for sexual love if one experiences it too early. The fine homily on Love and Lust (like the love-persuasions of Marlowe's Leander) comes oddly from one so innocent, and the inconsistency is not removed by the fact that Adonis admits it (806).

In addition to such distortions of character, which Shakespeare seems to have permitted himself for the sake of immediate effects, the reader must cope with apparent shifts in the poet's attitude toward his material. It will be granted, I am sure, that comedy enters the poem at the end of stanza 5, where Venus pulls Adonis from his horse and lugs him off under her arm, blushing and pouting. We are amused because a female is manhandling a male, and because the goddess of Love (though later she will stress her weightlessness) here seems not merely Rubenesque but grotesquely muscular. The occurrence is a sexual assault which, if described in a different key, might invite prurience and encourage perverse or passive fantasy. But there is no Swinburnian heavy breathing here; it is vaudeville, and it is vaudeville when Venus later falls flat not once but twice (463, 593).

If the presence of broad comedy forbids a prurient response to the early stanzas, the element of slapstick is in turn refined by the graceful artifice of Venus' entreaties, by her persistent high idealization of Adonis' beauty, by Shakespeare's stress on the loveliness of Adonis' "pretty ear" or Venus' "fair immortal hand," and by the benign ambience of summer dawn. We cannot take the word "lust" very seriously in an atmosphere of violets and dive-dappers; and when Venus "devours" Adonis as an eagle its prey, we are less likely to think of *Vénus tout entière à sa proie attachée* than of the amorous commonplace "I could eat you alive." The reader, in short, feels himself to be in that special literary preserve where the erotic may freely be enjoyed because taste and humor attend and control it. This is the domain of much of Herrick's poetry, and here as there it is understood that moral objections would be churlish.

A critic of 1823 described *Venus and Adonis* as "deficient in that delicacy which has happily been introduced by modern refinement." The eroticism of the poem, however, is never culpably gross. Venus' celebrated "deer park" speech (229 ff.) is far too clever for pornographic purposes, and such lines as the following have a Marlovian coolness and suavity:

> Who sees his true-love in her naked bed,
> Teaching the sheets a whiter hue than white,

> But, when his glutton eye so full hath fed,
> His other agents aim at like delight ?   (397-400)

There are also (in addition to the other alleviations I have mentioned) occasional maxims of this sort :

> Were beauty under twenty locks kept fast,
> Yet love breaks through and picks them all at last.
> (575-76)

This lacks the irony of Marlowe, but like his maxims in *Hero and Leander* it distances the action by amused generalization.

Nevertheless, Shakespeare's poem breaks its own contract with the reader. By line 551 Venus' eagle has become a vulture, her face "doth reek and smoke," and her "lust" is being denounced by the poet for its shamelessness and its subversion of reason. This passage endorses in advance Adonis' tirade (769 ff.) against "sweating Lust," in which that sweat which first seemed earthily matter-of-fact (25) and later erotically attractive (143-44) becomes wholly distasteful. Is the reader expected, at this point, to make such judgments retroactive, and to see the first part of the poem in a radically altered light ? If so, it is too much to ask. One could no more do it than one could reconceive *Macbeth* as comedy. Shakespeare's (and Adonis') distinctions between Love and Lust are in themselves eloquent and sound, but they have no place in such a poem as *Venus* started out to be, and one is forced to consider two possible explanations : either Shakespeare thought that he could jump, with aesthetic safety, from one Ovidian tradition to another ; or the poet who was soon to write Sonnet 129 ("Th' expense of spirit in a waste of shame / Is lust in action") could not temperamentally sustain a blithe and amoral approach to sexual love.

Some critics, unwilling that Shakespeare should seem imperfect even in "the first heir of" his invention, have tried to read *Venus* as a coherent moral allegory. It is not hard to guess what sort of thing such attempts would entail: the identification of Adonis with reason and ideal beauty, Venus with lust; the assumption that hunting is here, as in *A Midsummer Night's Dream*, a metaphor for the conquest of the irrational; the interpretation of Adonis' horse as ungoverned appetite running mad; the placing of special emphasis on all passages (such as 889 ff.) having to do with the hierarchy of the faculties; and so on. The poem would thus become a myth (rather like Marlowe's digression, in *Hero and Leander*, on the enmity of Love and the Fates) of the flight of true Love and Beauty to heaven – a myth in which the imperfection of love on earth is explained as the result of passion's incapacity to defer to reason. Having come so far, an allegorical interpreter might dare to construe, in accordance with his view of the poem, that dense complex of repeated images or symbols which we encounter from the first stanza onward: suns and moons and faces red or pale, hot or cold; eyebeams or sunbeams commercing with the several elements, and with earth or heaven. By the time one finds the fatal boar being condemned for a "downward eye" imperceptive of beauty (1105 ff.) one is aware that these recurrent motifs may indeed be driving at something; but the present writer is unable, thus far, to resolve them into any structure, and finds that the chief result of so many burning faces, eyes, tears, and exhalations is an impression of close-up photography.

We are all, I hope, ambitious for Shakespeare, and would be pleased if the discovery of consistent moral allegory in his poem could be made in better conscience – with less suppression and inflation of evidence, and less disregard of tone. The moral and allegorical elements are really there; unfortunately, they are fitful and vague. It would please us, too, if the poem could be shown to have a clear pattern of attitudes embodied in its prevalent symbols; we might then hope to discover deep and powerful focal passages, as in the plays. The suns, moons, heads, and coins of *1 Henry IV*, and their attendant political conceptions, have such cumulative effect upon the reader's imagination that when, in Act IV, the Prince's troops are seen approaching Shrewsbury, "Glittering in golden coats like images . . . / And gorgeous as the sun at midsummer," those few words render the whole play simultaneous, and reverberate through all its architecture. But *Venus* is not architectural; there are no moments in which the entire work is many-dimensionally presented to the mind through a concentrative use of symbol or idea. The poem is additive, linear, spasmodic, opportunistic; it resembles a medieval episodic painting, or a series of tapestry panels deriving from one story but only tenuously related to each other. Or, to use a comparison nearer to our experience, it is like those musical comedies of the 1920's in which the "book" was a series of casual excuses for songs and dances, and the least mention of Chicago was sufficient to motivate a massive Chicago Number.

In order to enjoy *Venus and Adonis,* one must accept it as a lesser and looser thing than the more familiar plays, and not waste too much time in clucking one's tongue over its "frigid artificiality," its "remoteness from life," its deficiencies in story, character, and idea. The pleasures of the poem may be found anywhere at random, as in these lines from Venus' three-stanza vaunt about her conquest of Mars:

> Over my altars hath he hung his lance,
> His batt'red shield, his uncontrollèd crest,
> And for my sake hath learned to sport and dance,
> To toy, to wanton, dally, smile, and jest,
>   Scorning his churlish drum and ensign red,
>   Making my arms his field, his tent my bed.

(103–8)

That is part of an eighteen-line development of the paradox that the god of war should surrender. Both in *Venus* and in *Lucrece* Shakespeare sometimes employs brisk and arresting paradoxes ("O modest wantons, wanton modesty!"), but the relish of this passage lies in an eloquent expansion of the paradox, and a continually varied attack upon it. Wit is not always brief; Venus offers Adonis "Ten kisses short as one, one long as twenty," and Shakespeare knows that in witty verse one must similarly divert by unexpected proportion and duration. In the early poems, where subtlety is chiefly of the surface, he inclines to surprise more by excess than by concision, and we respond not with a jarred delight but with that growing wonder we feel when the still-strong miler lets himself out in the stretch, or the jazz trumpeter sails on into yet another chorus. We enjoy the display of resources, the prodigality, the abundance. In the stanza above, there is a fairly full inventory of Martial properties – lance, shield, helmet, drum, ensign, field, and tent; but these things are so variously tucked into the grammar as to give no impression of padding or of tiresome catalogue. And it is precisely this handling of one enumeration which permits another (the rather redundant infinitives of lines 105 and 106) to be contrastingly presented in bald sequence.

No reader with an ear can fail to note that the vowel-progressions of the stanza are melodious, and that the line, though end-stopped, is highly versatile in pace and rhythm; the movement of the whole is nervously fluent, as suits an extended poem so decoratively aloof from action and drama. It will be noticed here, as in the poem generally, that Shakespeare's lines tend to contain words, or groups of words, which balance upon some principle or other: very often, as in a line I have quoted ("The foul boar's conquest on her fair delight"), the balance involves antithesis. Line 104 above represents "balancing" at its most obvious, but in line 107 we have something subtler: a strong initial verb defers the seesaw effect, and the balanced words are inversely arranged as adjective-noun and noun-adjective. Line 108 then cleverly repeats the pattern with other grammatical elements.

Such talk is exceedingly dry, but it does bear upon the main and steadiest sources of pleasure in the poem – for us as for the artifice-loving Elizabethans: its elaborate inventiveness, its rhetorical dexterity, its technical *éclat*. There are numerous moments at which the poem creates a response to its subject, as in the beautiful stanza of the hands (361 ff.), but mostly one is reacting to an ostentatious poetic performance the artful variety of which I have scarcely begun to describe. Shakespeare has used an Ovidian story as the basis, not of a narrative, dramatic, or philosophic poem, but of a concatenation of virtuoso descriptions, comparisons, apostrophes, essays, pleas, reproaches, digressions, laments, and what have you. The same is true of *Lucrece*, that "graver labor" which Shakespeare promised in his dedication of *Venus*, and which he published a year later, in 1594.

In this case the Ovidian source is the *Fasti*, and again Shakespeare was working with a story which English writers (among them Chaucer) had helped to make familiar. A prose "argument," and a first stanza which starts the action well along in the plot, serve to curtail the narrative, and the 1855-line poem will really tell or show us only this: the inner struggles of Tarquin as he approaches Lucrece's bed; his threatening proposal, and her pleas and refusals; her lamentations, once she has been dishonored; her revelation of Tarquin's guilt to Collatine and others; her suicide, and the banishment of the Tarquins. A very large part of the poem consists of solitary lamentation by Lucrece, and it is undoubtedly true that Shakespeare was here creating a hybrid genre by combining a species of Ovidian narrative with the "complaint": it was probably from Daniel's *Complaint of Rosamond* (1593), in which the ghost of Henry II's unfortunate mistress asks our prayers and pity, that Shakespeare borrowed the stately 7-line stanza of *Lucrece*. At the same time, *Lucrece* greatly differs from *Rosamond*, the latter being a first-person account which offers neither

scene nor dialogue until the poem is two-thirds done. Like
Venus, Lucrece is narrated by the poet; it has access to the
thoughts of its two principals, and consists in great part of
rhetorical speeches which may at times suggest declama-
tory or Senecan drama, but seldom suggest that the poet
has a future in the theatre. Critics agree that among the
few moments of dramatic potentiality are those in which
Lucrece countermands her agitated orders to her maid
(1289 ff.) and misunderstands the blushes of her groom
(1338 ff.). One also feels that the reunion of Lucrece and
her husband might be touching on the stage:

> Both stood, like old acquaintance in a trance,
> Met far from home, wond'ring each other's chance.
> (1595–96)

Action in *Lucrece* is smothered in poetry, as when the
concrete effect of Tarquin's lifted sword (505) is instantly
blunted by a comparison; moreover, the action is given us
in disjunct and unresolved tableaux. The sword is never
lowered, and the hand remains indefinitely on the breast.
Our mind's eye beholds not a cinematic continuity, but
slides or tapestries which description may explore (as
Lucrece explores her painting of Troy) or rhetoric at once
forsake. Ideas are unimportant; the poet is not out to
demonstrate the nature of chastity, or to confront the
problem of evil in the world; his thought is conventional
and can often be rendered by proverbs. Character in
Lucrece is shallow, fixed, yet inconsistent, as in *Venus and
Adonis*, and for the same reason: it is brilliance of the surface which has priority. Thus Tarquin is at first the
"devil" to Lucrece's "saint" (85), but once alone and
pondering he is provided with a better nature, so that he
may be torn between conscience and lust; and this is done
not for the sake of psychological revelation but for the pro-
vision of antithesis and rhetorical opportunity. Lucrece,
when contemplating suicide, takes temporarily the Chris-
tian view of self-slaughter (1156 ff.) in order to divide

herself for three stanzas. Divisions, vacillations, inward debates, anatomies of stimulus and response (426 ff.) and of psychic politics (288 ff.) – the poem is full of these things, and their main *raison d'être* is stylistic: they break down the characters and their thoughts into elements which can be balanced and elaborated.

The verse of *Lucrece* is even more obtrusively artificial than that of *Venus*, and its trickiness is somehow more difficult to like. Our first view of the heroine consists of a 28-line description of the "war of lilies and of roses" in her complexion (50–77), and its length and difficulty are exasperatingly disproportionate to the content. Perhaps the subject and initial tone of *Venus* make its extravagances – the egregious dimples of 241–48, for example – seem forgivably playful, while in a grave poem about rape and suicide such fiddling with red and white seems Neronian. There are, however, passages to admire, especially in the linked lamentations of Lucrece, which flow into each other with a smoothness worthy of Ovid. In contrast to Ovid and the Ovidians, Shakespeare makes little use, either in *Venus* or in *Lucrece*, of mythological reference, but when Lucrece invites Philomel to a duet (1128 ff.) a most obvious comparison of fates is made with the utmost freshness. And – to praise one passage more – Lucrece's contemplation of the painting of Troy is far more than a standard Elizabethan descriptive exercise, written to occupy the interval between the sending of the scroll and Collatine's return. It is, for one thing, full of explicit and implicit relationships between Troy and Lucrece's Rome. We are to liken Ardea's siege to Troy's; Helen in her "rape" resembles Lucrece, but in her infidelity contrasts with her; Paris, like Tarquin, is a king's son who puts his "private pleasure" before the public good; Sinon, like Tarquin, is a dissimulator, and the entry of the Greek horse into Troy is like Tarquin's ill-intentioned entry into Collatine's house. The description is also relevant to Tarquin's moral collapse, in its several contrasts between displays of passion (such as anger or cowardice) and examples of "government" or control. Finally, the passage dwells considerably on the clear depiction and ready perception of character or emotion in physiognomy, and so builds throughout toward Lucrece's bitter reflection that such a face as Tarquin's can yet "bear a wicked mind."

I have left myself scarcely any space in which to speak of that strange and masterly metaphysical poem, "The Phoenix and Turtle." Published in 1601, the poem is a celebration of ideal love between two people, its perfect lovers being presented as symbolic birds, the phoenix and the turtledove. Poets have often made *ad hoc* revisions of mythology or conventional symbolism, and Shakespeare has done so here: while the turtledove keeps its accepted meaning of Constancy, the phoenix is assigned the feminine gender and is made to stand not for Immortality, as would be traditional, but for Love. These initial attributions, however, are in no way limiting, for since the two birds accomplish a total fusion of their natures, they have at last the one joint meaning of pure and imperishable love. The poem is undoubtedly indebted to other literary bird-assemblies, such as Chaucer's *Parliament of Fowls,* but given the chaste and world-forsaking character of the love whereby they are translated "In a mutual flame from hence," I think that the lovers must owe something of their wingedness to the *Phaedrus.* There Plato describes the highest love as an absolute spiritual union through which the lovers' souls recover their lost wings, and "when the end comes . . . are light and winged for flight."

The first part of the poem, in which the phoenix and turtle go unmentioned, is a summons to the celebrants and worthy witnesses of their funeral rite. The second part, which begins at the sixth stanza, is an anthem of praise in which those assembled "chaste wings" approach the transcendent truth of ideal love by demonstrating the powerlessness of reason to describe it: that two souls should be one is an idea which defeats mathematics and logic, and forces language into violent paradox. The collective reason of the mourners, convinced by self-defeat that "Love hath reason, reason none," proceeds then to compose a "threne" or dirge which is the poem's third movement. In it, reason affirms that the lovers have embodied a truth which lies beyond reason, and which with their death is lost to the world; at the same time, in response to the spirit of renewal which concludes all obsequies, and to the phoenix's association with the idea of rebirth, the "true or fair" are quietly made heirs of the lovers' example.

The language of this poem is intellectually strict and dry; the rhythm is abrupt and rugged in the tetrameter quatrains, like that of a nursery rhyme, and just a shade more serene in the triplets of the *Threnos*. The product of this precise abstract language and these spirited trochaic lines is, for one reader at least, an impression of complete vitality. We need not ask, in this poem, what and how much is meant by predatory birds or by burning eyes; the meanings are strong and ultimately plain. The Platonic conception of love, which in *Venus and Adonis* was inchoate and momentary, is here sharply realized, and the gift of paradox, which in *Venus* and *Lucrece* was exercised for its own sake, here serves a theme which cannot be expressed without it.

Wesleyan University   RICHARD WILBUR

NOTE ON THE TEXTS

Venus and Adonis was first printed in quarto in 1593, and was often reprinted; *Lucrece* (with the head title *The Rape of Lucrece*) was first printed in quarto in 1594, and was reprinted a number of times, although less often than its predecessor. Both poems bear dedications to the Earl of Southampton subscribed "William Shakespeare," and both are well printed, probably from the author's fair copies. It is generally agreed that the later editions lack independent authority. "The Phoenix and Turtle" was first printed in a quarto of 1601: Robert Chester's *Love's Martyr, or Rosaline's Complaint*, a volume containing, besides the quaint verses of Chester himself, variations upon the theme of the Phoenix and Turtle "by the best and chiefest of our modern writers, with their names subscribed to their particular works, never before extant. And now first consecrated by them all generally to the love and merit of the true-noble knight, Sir John Salisbury." Of the cluster of poems thus described, two are signed "Vatum Chorus," one "Ignoto," one "William Shake-speare," one "John Marston," one "George Chapman," and two "Ben Jonson." Although reprinted, the original quarto of 1601 is the sole authority for the text. The present edition of the three poems is based on the text of the original quartos, with the following material emendations. The adopted reading in italics is followed by the quarto reading in roman.

VENUS AND ADONIS 19 *satiety* saciety 147 *dishevelled* di-shevellèd 358 *wooed* wooèd 366 *Showed* Showèd 432 *Ear's* Eares 616 *javelin's* iavelings 644 *Saw'st* Sawest 680 *overshoot* ouer-shut 754 *sons* suns 873 *twind* twin'd 940 *dost* doest 1003 *fault* fault, 1031 *as* are 1054 *was* had

THE RAPE OF LUCRECE (press-corrected Q) 23 *decayed* de-cayèd 50 *Collatium* (uncorrected Q) Colatia (corrected Q) 111 *heaved-up* heauèd-up 192, 392, 552 *unhallowed* vnhallowèd 395 *Showed* showèd 573, 1549 *borrowed* borrowèd 883 *mak'st* makest 884 *blow'st* blowest 1159 *swallowed* swallowèd 1416 *shadowed* shadowèd 1662 *wreathèd* wretchèd 1680 *one woe* on woe 1713 *in it* it in

The text and glossarial notes have been prepared by the general editor.

VENUS AND ADONIS

Vilia miretur vulgus : mihi flavus Apollo
Pocula Castalia plena ministret aqua.

TO THE RIGHT HONORABLE
2 # HENRY WRIOTHESLEY
EARL OF SOUTHAMPTON,
AND BARON OF TITCHFIELD

RIGHT HONORABLE,
    I know not how I shall offend in dedicating my un-
polished lines to your Lordship, nor how the world will
censure me for choosing so strong a prop to support so
weak a burden; only, if your Honor seem but pleased, I
account myself highly praised, and vow to take advantage
of all idle hours, till I have honored you with some graver
12 labor. But if the first heir of my invention prove deformed,
I shall be sorry it had so noble a godfather, and never after
14 ear so barren a land, for fear it yield me still so bad a
harvest. I leave it to your honorable survey, and your
Honor to your heart's content; which I wish may always
answer your own wish and the world's hopeful expecta-
tion.

Your Honor's in all duty,
WILLIAM SHAKESPEARE

Vilia . . . aqua (from Ovid's *Amores*, I, xv, 35–36: Let the cheap dazzle
the crowd; for me, may golden Apollo minister full cups from the Cas-
talian spring) Ded., 2 *Henry Wriothesley* third Earl of Southampton,
1573–1624, a favorite at the court of Elizabeth until imprisoned, 1601–03,
for complicity in the Essex Rebellion 12 *first . . . invention* i.e. first work of
literary pretensions? (since a number of plays had already been written)
14 *ear* cultivate, till

VENUS AND ADONIS

Even as the sun with purple-colored face 1
Had ta'en his last leave of the weeping morn,
Rose-cheeked Adonis hied him to the chase.
Hunting he loved, but love he laughed to scorn.
    Sick-thoughted Venus makes amain unto him 5
    And like a bold-faced suitor 'gins to woo him.

'Thrice fairer than myself,' thus she began,
'The field's chief flower, sweet above compare,
Stain to all nymphs, more lovely than a man,
More white and red than doves or roses are, 9
    Nature that made thee, with herself at strife, 11
    Saith that the world hath ending with thy life.

'Vouchsafe, thou wonder, to alight thy steed,
And rein his proud head to the saddlebow.
If thou wilt deign this favor, for thy meed
A thousand honey secrets shalt thou know.
    Here come and sit, where never serpent hisses
    And being set, I'll smother thee with kisses.

1 *purple-colored* i.e. crimson ('purple' being used for a considerable range of colors) 5 *Sick-thoughted* i.e. suffering from love-melancholy 9 *Stain . . . nymphs* i.e. making all nymphs suffer by comparison 11 *with . . . strife* i.e. striving to outdo herself

'And yet not cloy thy lips with loathed satiety,
But rather famish them amid their plenty,
21   Making them red and pale with fresh variety –
Ten kisses short as one, one long as twenty.
    A summer's day will seem an hour but short,
24   Being wasted in such time-beguiling sport.'

25   With this she seizeth on his sweating palm,
26   The precedent of pith and livelihood,
And trembling in her passion, calls it balm,
Earth's sovereign salve to do a goddess good.
29   Being so enraged, desire doth lend her force
    Courageously to pluck him from his horse.

Over one arm the lusty courser's rein,
Under her other was the tender boy,
Who blushed and pouted in a dull disdain,
With leaden appetite, unapt to toy;
    She red and hot as coals of glowing fire,
    He red for shame, but frosty in desire.

The studded bridle on a ragged bough
Nimbly she fastens. O, how quick is love!
The steed is stallèd up, and even now
40   To tie the rider she begins to prove.
    Backward she pushed him, as she would be thrust,
    And governed him in strength, though not in lust.

21 *Making . . . pale* i.e. alternately suffused with and drained of blood
24 *wasted* spent   25 *sweating* i.e. not parched, youthful   26 *precedent*
promise, sign; *pith and livelihood* strength and vitality   29 *enraged* aroused
40 *prove* try

So soon was she along as he was down,   43
Each leaning on their elbows and their hips.
Now doth she stroke his cheek, now doth he frown
And 'gins to chide; but soon she stops his lips
 And kissing speaks, with lustful language broken,
 'If thou wilt chide, thy lips shall never open.'

He burns with bashful shame; she with her tears
Doth quench the maiden burning of his cheeks.
Then with her windy sighs and golden hairs
To fan and blow them dry again she seeks.
 He saith she is immodest, blames her miss;   53
 What follows more she murders with a kiss.

Even as an empty eagle, sharp by fast,   55
Tires with her beak on feathers, flesh, and bone,   56
Shaking her wings, devouring all in haste,
Till either gorge be stuffed or prey be gone –
 Even so she kissed his brow, his cheek, his chin,
 And where she ends she doth anew begin.

Forced to content, but never to obey,   61
Panting he lies and breatheth in her face.
She feedeth on the steam as on a prey
And calls it heavenly moisture, air of grace,
 Wishing her cheeks were gardens full of flowers,
 So they were dewed with such distilling showers.

43 *along* beside him   53 *miss* misbehavior   55 *sharp by fast* hungry from
fasting   56 *Tires* preys hungrily   61 *content* i.e. put up with it

Look how a bird lies tangled in a net,
So fast'ned in her arms Adonis lies.
69 Pure shame and awed resistance made him fret,
Which bred more beauty in his angry eyes.
71   Rain added to a river that is rank
    Perforce will force it overflow the bank.

Still she entreats, and prettily entreats,
74 For to a pretty ear she tunes her tale.
Still is he sullen, still he low'rs and frets,
'Twixt crimson shame and anger ashy-pale.
    Being red, she loves him best; and being white,
78   Her best is bettered with a more delight.

Look how he can, she cannot choose but love;
And by her fair immortal hand she swears
From his soft bosom never to remove
82 Till he take truce with her contending tears,
    Which long have rained, making her cheeks all wet;
84   And one sweet kiss shall pay this comptless debt.

Upon this promise did he raise his chin,
86 Like a divedapper peering through a wave,
Who, being looked on, ducks as quickly in.
So offers he to give what she did crave;
    But when her lips were ready for his pay,
90   He winks and turns his lips another way.

69 *awed* overborne   71 *rank* teeming   74 *ear* (punning on 'air')   78 *more*
greater   82 *take truce* make peace   84 *comptless* countless   86 *divedapper*
dabchick, little grebe   90 *winks* shuts his eyes

Never did passenger in summer's heat   91
More thirst for drink than she for this good turn.
Her help she sees, but help she cannot get;
She bathes in water, yet her fire must burn.
    'O, pity,' 'gan she cry, 'flint-hearted boy!
    'Tis but a kiss I beg – why are thou coy?

'I have been wooed, as I entreat thee now,
Even by the stern and direful god of war,
Whose sinewy neck in battle ne'er did bow,
Who conquers where he comes in every jar;   100
    Yet hath he been my captive and my slave,
    And begged for that which thou unasked shalt have.

'Over my altars hath he hung his lance,
His batt'red shield, his uncontrollèd crest,   104
And for my sake hath learned to sport and dance,
To toy, to wanton, dally, smile, and jest,
    Scorning his churlish drum and ensign red,
    Making my arms his field, his tent my bed.

'Thus he that overruled I overswayèd,
Leading him prisoner in a red-rose chain.
Strong-tempered steel his stronger strength obeyèd;
Yet was he servile to my coy disdain.
    O, be not proud, nor brag not of thy might,
    For mast'ring her that foiled the god of fight!

91 *passenger* wayfarer   **100** *jar* fight   **104** *uncontrollèd crest* unbowed helmet

'Touch but my lips with those fair lips of thine –
Though mine be not so fair, yet are they red –
The kiss shall be thine own as well as mine.
What seest thou in the ground ? Hold up thy head.
    Look in mine eyeballs, there thy beauty lies,
    Then why not lips on lips, since eyes in eyes ?

121   'Art thou ashamed to kiss ? Then wink again,
122   And I will wink – so shall the day seem night.
       Love keeps his revels where there are but twain.
124   Be bold to play ; our sport is not in sight.
       These blue-veined violets whereon we lean
126   Never can blab, nor know not what we mean.

127   'The tender spring upon thy tempting lip
       Shows thee unripe ; yet mayst thou well be tasted.
129   Make use of time, let not advantage slip ;
130   Beauty within itself should not be wasted.
       Fair flowers that are not gath'red in their prime
       Rot and consume themselves in little time.

133   'Were I hard-favored, foul, or wrinkled old,
       Ill-nurtured, crooked, churlish, harsh in voice,
135   O'erworn, despisèd, rheumatic, and cold,
136   Thick-sighted, barren, lean and lacking juice
       Then mightst thou pause, for then I were not for thee ;
       But having no defects, why dost abhor me ?

121, 122 *wink* shut eyes   124 *not in sight* i.e. unseen   126 *blab* tell tales; *nor know not* i.e. or know; *mean* intend to do   127 *tender spring* i.e. light down 129 *advantage* opportunity   130 *within itself* i.e. buried in itself   133 *foul* ugly   135 *O'erworn* jaded   136 *Thick-sighted* dull of sight

'Thou canst not see one wrinkle in my brow;
Mine eyes are grey and bright and quick in turning;   140
My beauty as the spring doth yearly grow,
My flesh is soft and plump, my marrow burning;
  My smooth moist hand, were it with thy hand felt,
  Would in thy palm dissolve or seem to melt.

'Bid me discourse, I will enchant thine ear,
Or, like a fairy, trip upon the green,
Or, like a nymph, with long dishevelled hair,
Dance on the sands, and yet no footing seen.   148
  Love is a spirit all compact of fire,   149
  Not gross to sink, but light, and will aspire.

'Witness this primrose bank whereon I lie;
These forceless flowers like sturdy trees support me.   152
Two strengthless doves will draw me through the sky
From morn till night, even where I list to sport me.
  Is love so light, sweet boy, and may it be
  That thou should think it heavy unto thee?

'Is thine own heart to thine own face affected?   157
Can thy right hand seize love upon thy left?   158
Then woo thyself, be of thyself rejected;
Steal thine own freedom, and complain on theft.
  Narcissus so himself himself forsook.   161
  And died to kiss his shadow in the brook.

---

140 *grey* (used of a range of iris-coloring which included blue)   **148** *footing* footprint   **149** *compact* composed   **152** *forceless* without strength   **157** *affected* devoted   **158** *upon thy left* i.e. by clasping your left hand   **161** *Narcissus* in classical myth, the youth in love with his own image and transformed into the narcissus

'Torches are made to light, jewels to wear,
Dainties to taste, fresh beauty for the use,
Herbs for their smell, and sappy plants to bear.
166 Things growing to themselves are growth's abuse.
  Seeds spring from seeds, and beauty breedeth beauty.
  Thou wast begot; to get it is thy duty.

169 'Upon the earth's increase why shouldst thou feed
Unless the earth with thy increase be fed?
By law of nature thou art bound to breed,
That thine may live when thou thyself art dead;
  And so, in spite of death, thou dost survive,
  In that thy likeness still is left alive.'

By this, the lovesick queen began to sweat,
For where they lay the shadow had forsook them,
177 And Titan, tirèd in the midday heat,
With burning eye did hotly over-look them,
  Wishing Adonis had his team to guide,
180 So he were like him, and by Venus' side.

181 And now Adonis, with a lazy sprite,
And with a heavy, dark, disliking eye,
His low'ring brows o'erwhelming his fair sight,
Like misty vapors when they blot the sky,
  Souring his cheeks, cries, 'Fie, no more of love!
  The sun doth burn my face – I must remove.'

---

166 *to* for (i.e. with no other purpose but growth) 169 *increase* harvest
177 *Titan* the sun-god; *tirèd* attired 180 *he* i.e. Titan 181 *lazy sprite* dull
spirit

'Ay me,' quoth Venus, 'young, and so unkind?
What bare excuses mak'st thou to be gone!
I'll sigh celestial breath, whose gentle wind
Shall cool the heat of this descending sun.
  I'll make a shadow for thee of my hairs;
  If they burn too, I'll quench them with my tears.

'The sun that shines from heaven shines but warm;
And, lo, I lie between that sun and thee.
The heat I have from thence doth little harm;
Thine eye darts forth the fire that burneth me,
  And were I not immortal, life were done
  Between this heavenly and earthly sun.

'Art thou obdurate, flinty, hard as steel?
Nay, more than flint, for stone at rain relenteth.   200
Art thou a woman's son, and canst not feel
What 'tis to love? how want of love tormenteth?
  O, had thy mother borne so hard a mind,
  She had not brought forth thee, but died unkind.

'What am I that thou shouldst contemn me this?   205
Or what great danger dwells upon my suit?   206
What were thy lips the worse for one poor kiss?
Speak, fair, but speak fair words or else be mute.
  Give me one kiss, I'll give it thee again,
  And one for int'rest, if thou wilt have twain.

200 *relenteth* yields, is worn away   205 *this* thus (old form)   206 *dwells upon* attends

33

'Fie, liveless picture, cold and senseless stone,
Well-painted idol, image dull and dead,
Statue contenting but the eye alone,
Thing like a man, but of no woman bred!
   Thou art no man, though of a man's complexion,
216   For men will kiss even by their own direction.'

This said, impatience chokes her pleading tongue,
And swelling passion doth provoke a pause;
Red cheeks and fiery eyes blaze forth her wrong:
220 Being judge in love, she cannot right her cause,
   And now she weeps, and now she fain would speak,
222   And now her sobs do her intendments break.

Sometime she shakes her head, and then his hand;
Now gazeth she on him, now on the ground;
Sometime her arms infold him like a band –
She would, he will not in her arms be bound;
   And when from thence he struggles to be gone,
    She locks her lily fingers one in one.

229 'Fondling,' she saith, 'since I have hemmed thee here
230 Within the circuit of this ivory pale,
231 I'll be a park, and thou shalt be my deer:
   Feed where thou wilt, on mountain or in dale;
    Graze on my lips; and if those hills be dry,
    Stray lower, where the pleasant fountains lie.

---

216 *by . . . direction* i.e. without prompting 220 *Being . . . cause* i.e. Venus, although presiding over the court of love, cannot obtain a favorable verdict in her own case 222 *do . . . break* frustrate her intentions 229 *Fondling* fondled one, darling (?), cause of infatuation (?) 230 *pale* fence 231 *park* deer-preserve

'Within this limit is relief enough,   235
Sweet bottom-grass, and high delightful plain,   236
Round rising hillocks, brakes obscure and rough,   237
To shelter thee from tempest and from rain.
   Then be my deer, since I am such a park.
   No dog shall rouse thee, though a thousand bark.'   240

At this Adonis smiles as in disdain,
That in each cheek appears a pretty dimple.   242
Love made those hollows, if himself were slain,   243
He might be buried in a tomb so simple,   244
   Foreknowing well, if there he came to lie,
   Why, there Love lived, and there he could not die.

These lovely caves, these round enchanting pits,
Opened their mouths to swallow Venus' liking.
Being mad before, how doth she now for wits?   249
Struck dead at first, what needs a second striking?
   Poor queen of love, in thine own law forlorn,   251
   To love a cheek that smiles at thee in scorn!

Now which way shall she turn? what shall she say?
Her words are done, her woes the more increasing;
The time is spent, her object will away,
And from her twining arms doth urge releasing.
   'Pity!' she cries, 'Some favor, some remorse!'   257
   Away he springs and hasteth to his horse.

---

235 *limit* boundary **236** *bottom-grass* valley-grass **237** *brakes* thickets
240 *rouse* start **242** *That* so that **243** *if* so that if **244** *tomb* i.e. grave
249 *how . . . wits* i.e. how keep her sanity now **251** *in . . . forlorn* wretched
under your own rule (of love) **257** *remorse* pity

But, lo, from forth a copse that neighbors by
260 A breeding jennet, lusty, young, and proud,
Adonis' trampling courser doth espy,
And forth she rushes, snorts, and neighs aloud.
 The strong-necked steed, being tied unto a tree,
 Breaketh his rein, and to her straight goes he.

Imperiously he leaps, he neighs, he bounds,
And now his woven girths he breaks asunder;
267 The bearing earth with his hard hoof he wounds,
Whose hollow womb resounds like heaven's thunder;
 The iron bit he crusheth 'tween his teeth,
 Controlling what he was controllèd with.

His ears up-pricked; his braided hanging mane
272 Upon his compassed crest now stand on end;
His nostrils drink the air, and forth again,
As from a furnace, vapors doth he send;
275 His eye, which scornfully glisters like fire,
276 Shows his hot courage and his high desire.

277 Sometime he trots, as if he told the steps,
With gentle majesty and modest pride;
Anon he rears upright, curvets, and leaps,
As who should say, 'Lo, thus my strength is tried,
 And this I do to captivate the eye
 Of the fair breeder that is standing by.'

260 *jennet* small Spanish horse 267 *bearing* receiving 272 *compassed*
arched 275 *scornfully glisters* (perhaps transposed by printer) 276
courage passion 277 *told* counted

What recketh he his rider's angry stir,   283
His flattering 'Holla' or his 'Stand, I say'?   284
What cares he now for curb or pricking spur?
For rich caparisons or trappings gay?
    He sees his love, and nothing else he sees,
    For nothing else with his proud sight agrees.

Look when a painter would surpass the life   289
In limning out a well-proportionèd steed,   290
His art with nature's workmanship at strife,
As if the dead the living should exceed –   292
    So did this horse excel a common one
    In shape, in courage, color, pace, and bone.   294

Round-hoofed, short-jointed, fetlocks shag and long, 295
Broad breast, full eye, small head, and nostril wide,
High crest, short ears, straight legs and passing strong, 297
Thin mane, thick tail, broad buttock, tender hide:
    Look what a horse should have he did not lack, 299
    Save a proud rider on so proud a back.

Sometimes he scuds far off, and there he stares;
Anon he starts at stirring of a feather;
To bid the wind a base he now prepares,   303
And where he run or fly they know not whether, 304
    For through his mane and tail the high wind sings,
    Fanning the hairs, who wave like feath'red wings.

283 *stir* bustle 284 *flattering* soothing 289 *Look when* as when 290 *limning out* portraying 292 *dead* i.e. lifeless image 294 *bone* frame 295 *shag* bushy 297 *crest* ridge of the neck 299 *Look what* whatever 303 *bid . . . base* i.e. challenge the wind to outrun him or be taken prisoner (as in game of prisoner's base) 304 *where* whether

He looks upon his love and neighs unto her;
She answers him, as if she knew his mind.
Being proud, as females are, to see him woo her,
310 She puts on outward strangeness, seems unkind,
  Spurns at his love and scorns the heat he feels,
  Beating his kind embracements with her heels.

Then, like a melancholy malcontent,
314 He vails his tail, that, like a falling plume,
Cool shadow to his melting buttock lent;
316 He stamps, and bites the poor flies in his fume.
  His love, perceiving how he is enraged,
  Grew kinder, and his fury was assuaged.

His testy master goeth about to take him,
320 When, lo, the unbacked breeder, full of fear,
321 Jealous of catching, swiftly doth forsake him,
322 With her the horse, and left Adonis there.
  As they were mad, unto the woods they hie them,
324 Outstripping crows that strive to overfly them.

All swol'n with chafing, down Adonis sits,
326 Banning his boist'rous and unruly beast;
And now the happy season once more fits
328 That lovesick Love by pleading may be blest;
  For lovers say the heart hath treble wrong
  When it is barred the aidance of the tongue.

310 *outward strangeness* show of coyness   314 *vails* lowers   316 *fume* rage
320 *unbacked* unridden, unbroken   321 *Jealous of catching* fearful of being
caught   322 *horse* i.e. stallion   324 *overfly them* i.e. remain over them in
flight   326 *Banning* cursing   328 *Love* i.e. Venus

An oven that is stopped, or river stayed,   331
Burneth more hotly, swelleth with more rage;
So of concealèd sorrow may be said:
Free vent of words love's fire doth assuage;
    But when the heart's attorney once is mute,   335
    The client breaks, as desperate in his suit.   336

He sees her coming and begins to glow,
Even as a dying coal revives with wind,
And with his bonnet hides his angry brow,
Looks on the dull earth with disturbèd mind,
    Taking no notice that she is so nigh,
    For all askance he holds her in his eye.

O, what a sight it was, wistly to view   343
How she came stealing to the wayward boy!
To note the fighting conflict of her hue,
How white and red each other did destroy!
    But now her cheek was pale, and by and by
    It flashed forth fire, as lightning from the sky.

Now was she just before him as he sat,
And like a lowly lover down she kneels;
With one fair hand she heaveth up his hat,
Her other tender hand his fair cheek feels.
    His tend'rer cheek receives her soft hand's print
    As apt as new-fall'n snow takes any dint.   354

---

331 *stopped* i.e. with door closed; *stayed* i.e. dammed   335 *attorney* pleader
336 *breaks* goes bankrupt   343 *wistly* intently   354 *dint* impression

O, what a war of looks was then between them,
Her eyes petitioners to his eyes suing!
357   His eyes saw her eyes as they had not seen them;
Her eyes wooed still, his eyes disdained the wooing;
359   And all this dumb play had his acts made plain
360   With tears which chorus-like her eyes did rain.

Full gently now she takes him by the hand,
A lily prisoned in a jail of snow,
363   Or ivory in an alablaster band –
So white a friend engirts so white a foe.
    This beauteous combat, willful and unwilling,
    Showed like two silver doves that sit a-billing.

367   Once more the engine of her thoughts began:
368   'O fairest mover on this mortal round,
Would thou wert as I am, and I a man,
370   My heart all whole as thine, thy heart my wound!
    For one sweet look thy help I would assure thee,
372   Though nothing but my body's bane would cure thee.'

'Give me my hand,' saith he. 'Why dost thou feel it?'
'Give me my heart,' saith she, 'and thou shalt have it.
375   O, give it me, lest thy hard heart do steel it,
376   And being steeled, soft sighs can never grave it.
    Then love's deep groans I never shall regard,
    Because Adonis' heart hath made mine hard.'

---

357 *as* as if 359 *dumb play* dumbshow, wordless drama; *his* its 360 *chorus-like* i.e. as a commentary 363 *band* bond 367 *engine* instrument, i.e. tongue 368 *mortal round* i.e. earth 370 *my wound* i.e. wounded like mine 372 *bane* death by poison 375 *steel* turn to steel 376 *grave* engrave

'For shame!' he cries. 'Let go, and let me go:
My day's delight is past, my horse is gone,
And 'tis your fault I am bereft him so.
I pray you hence, and leave me here alone;
    For all my mind, my thought, my busy care
    Is how to get my palfrey from the mare.'

Thus she replies: 'Thy palfrey, as he should,
Welcomes the warm approach of sweet desire.
Affection is a coal that must be cooled;   387
Else, suffered, it will set the heart on fire.   388
    The sea hath bounds, but deep desire hath none;
    Therefore no marvel though thy horse be gone.

'How like a jade he stood, tied to the tree,
Servilely mastered with a leathern rein;
But when he saw his love, his youth's fair fee,   393
He held such petty bondage in disdain,
    Throwing the base thong from his bending crest,
    Enfranchising his mouth, his back, his breast.   396

'Who sees his true-love in her naked bed,
Teaching the sheets a whiter hue than white,
But, when his glutton eye so full hath fed,
His other agents aim at like delight?   400
    Who is so faint that dares not be so bold
    To touch the fire, the weather being cold?

---

387 *Affection* passion   388 *suffered* disregarded   393 *fair fee* due reward
396 *Enfranchising* setting free   400 *agents* organs

'Let me excuse thy courser, gentle boy;
And learn of him, I heartily beseech thee,
To take advantage on presented joy.
Though I were dumb, yet his proceedings teach thee.
   O, learn to love! The lesson is but plain,
    And once made perfect, never lost again.'

'I know not love,' quoth he, 'nor will not know it,
Unless it be a boar, and then I chase it.
411 'Tis much to borrow, and I will not owe it.
412 My love to love is love but to disgrace it;
   For I have heard it is a life in death,
414   That laughs, and weeps, and all but with a breath.

'Who wears a garment shapeless and unfinished?
Who plucks the bud before one leaf put forth?
417 If springing things be any jot diminished,
They wither in their prime, prove nothing worth.
419   The colt that's backed and burdened being young
    Loseth his pride and never waxeth strong.

'You hurt my hand with wringing. Let us part,
422 And leave this idle theme, this bootless chat.
Remove your siege from my unyielding heart;
424 To love's alarms it will not ope the gate.
   Dismiss your vows, your feignèd tears, your flatt'ry;
426   For where a heart is hard they make no batt'ry.'

411 *borrow* take on as an obligation; *owe* own, have   412 *My . . . it* i.e. my only feeling about love is the desire to belittle it   414 *all but with a* all but in one   417 *springing* sprouting   419 *backed* ridden   422 *bootless* profitless   424 *alarms* attacks   426 *batt'ry* forced entrance

'What! canst thou talk?' quoth she. 'Hast thou a tongue?
O, would thou hadst not, or I had no hearing!
Thy mermaid's voice hath done me double wrong;   429
I had my load before, now pressed with bearing: 430
　　Melodious discord, heavenly tune harsh sounding,
　　Ear's deep-sweet music, and heart's deep-sore wounding.

'Had I no eyes but ears, my ears would love
That inward beauty and invisible;
Or were I deaf, thy outward parts would move
Each part in me that were but sensible.   436
　　Though neither eyes nor ears, to hear nor see,
　　Yet should I be in love by touching thee.

'Say that the sense of feeling were bereft me,
And that I could not see, nor hear, nor touch,
And nothing but the very smell were left me,
Yet would my love to thee be still as much;
　　For from the stillitory of thy face excelling   443
　　Comes breath perfumed that breedeth love by smelling.

'But, O, what banquet wert thou to the taste,
Being nurse and feeder of the other four!
Would they not wish the feast might ever last
And bid Suspicion double-lock the door,   448
　　Lest Jealousy, that sour unwelcome guest,
　　Should by his stealing in disturb the feast?'

429 *mermaid's* siren's 430 *pressed* oppressed, weighted down 436 *sensible* sensitive to impressions 443 *stillitory* still 448 *Suspicion* caution

Once more the ruby-colored portal opened
452 Which to his speech did honey passage yield;
Like a red morn, that ever yet betokened
Wrack to the seaman, tempest to the field,
   Sorrow to shepherds, woe unto the birds,
456   Gusts and foul flaws to herdmen and to herds.

This ill presage advisedly she marketh.
Even as the wind is hushed before it raineth,
459 Or as the wolf doth grin before he barketh,
Or as the berry breaks before it staineth,
   Or like the deadly bullet of a gun,
   His meaning struck her ere his words begun.

And at his look she flatly falleth down,
For looks kill love, and love by looks reviveth;
465 A smile recures the wounding of a frown.
466 But blessèd bankrout that by loss so thriveth!
467   The silly boy, believing she is dead,
   Claps her pale cheek till clapping makes it red,

And all amazed brake off his late intent,
For sharply he did think to reprehend her,
471 Which cunning love did wittily prevent.
472 Fair fall the wit that can so well defend her!
   For on the grass she lies as she were slain
   Till his breath breatheth life in her again.

---

452 *honey* honeyed, sweet   456 *flaws* squalls   459 *grin* bare its teeth   465
recures cures   466 *bankrout* bankrupt   467 *silly* unsophisticated   471
wittily cleverly   472 *Fair fall* fair fortune befall

He wrings her nose, he strikes her on the cheeks,
He bends her finger, holds her pulses hard,
He chafes her lips ; a thousand ways he seeks
To mend the hurt that his unkindness marred.   478
   He kisses her ; and she, by her good will,
   Will never rise, so he will kiss her still.

The night of sorrow now is turned to day :
Her two blue windows faintly she upheaveth,   482
Like the fair sun when in his fresh array
He cheers the morn and all the earth relieveth ;
   And as the bright sun glorifies the sky,
   So is her face illumined with her eye ;

Whose beams upon his hairless face are fixed,
As if from thence they borrowèd all their shine.
Were never four such lamps together mixed,
Had not his clouded with his brow's repine ;   490
   But hers, which through the crystal tears gave light,
   Shone like the moon in water seen by night.

'O, where am I ?' quoth she, 'in earth or heaven,
Or in the ocean drenched, or in the fire ?   494
What hour is this ? or morn or weary even ?
Do I delight to die, or life desire ?
   But now I lived, and life was death's annoy ;   497
   But now I died, and death was lively joy.

478 *marred* i.e. inflicted (in a forced antithesis with 'mended') 482 *blue windows* i.e. eyelids 490 *repine* repining, dissatisfaction 494 *drenched* immersed 497 *annoy* harm

'O, thou didst kill me, kill me once again!
500 Thy eyes' shrewd tutor, that hard heart of thine,
Hath taught them scornful tricks, and such disdain
That they have murd'red this poor heart of mine;
503   And these mine eyes, true leaders to their queen,
    But for thy piteous lips no more had seen.

'Long may they kiss each other, for this cure!
506 O, never let their crimson liveries wear;
507 And as they last, their verdure still endure,
To drive infection from the dangerous year;
509   That the stargazers, having writ on death,
    May say the plague is banished by thy breath.

'Pure lips, sweet seals in my soft lips imprinted,
512 What bargains may I make, still to be sealing?
To sell myself I can be well contented,
So thou wilt buy, and pay, and use good dealing;
515   Which purchase if thou make, for fear of slips
    Set thy seal manual on my wax-red lips.

'A thousand kisses buys my heart from me;
And pay them at thy leisure, one by one.
519 What is ten hundred touches unto thee?
520 Are they not quickly told and quickly gone?
    Say for nonpayment that the debt should double,
    Is twenty hundred kisses such a trouble?'

---

500 *shrewd* sharp   503 *queen* i.e. the heart   506 *liveries* vestments; *wear* wear out   507 *verdure* fresh foliage (such as was brought indoors as a fumigant)   509 *stargazers . . . death* i.e. astrologers having predicted an epidemic   512 *still* so as always   515 *slips* errors   519 *touches* i.e. kisses 520 *told* counted

46

'Fair queen,' quoth he, 'if any love you owe me,   523
Measure my strangeness with my unripe years.   524
Before I know myself, seek not to know me.
No fisher but the ungrown fry forbears.   526
    The mellow plum doth fall, the green sticks fast,
    Or being early plucked is sour to taste.

'Look, the world's comforter, with weary gait,   529
His day's hot task hath ended in the west;
The owl, night's herald, shrieks; 'tis very late;
The sheep are gone to fold, birds to their nest,
    And coal-black clouds that shadow heaven's light
    Do summon us to part and bid good night.

'Now let me say "Good night," and so say you.
If you will say so, you shall have a kiss.'
'Good night,' quoth she; and, ere he says 'Adieu,'
The honey fee of parting tend'red is:
    Her arms do lend his neck a sweet embrace;
    Incorporate then they seem; face grows to face;   540

Till breathless he disjoined, and backward drew   541
The heavenly moisture, that sweet coral mouth,
Whose precious taste her thirsty lips well knew,
Whereon they surfeit, yet complain on drouth.
    He with her plenty pressed, she faint with dearth,   545
    Their lips together glued, fall to the earth.

523 *owe* bear   524 *Measure . . . with* i.e. account for my reserve by   526
fry fish   529 *world's comforter* i.e. the sun   540 *Incorporate* joined in a
single body   541 *disjoined* i.e. ended the incorporate state   545 *pressed*
oppressed

Now quick desire hath caught the yielding prey,
And glutton-like she feeds, yet never filleth.
Her lips are conquerors, his lips obey,
550 Paying what ransom the insulter willeth;
551   Whose vulture thought doth pitch the price so high
    That she will draw his lips' rich treasure dry.

And having felt the sweetness of the spoil,
With blindfold fury she begins to forage.
555 Her face doth reek and smoke, her blood doth boil,
And careless lust stirs up a desperate courage,
557   Planting oblivion, beating reason back,
558   Forgetting shame's pure blush and honor's wrack.

Hot, faint, and weary with her hard embracing,
Like a wild bird being tamed with too much handling,
Or as the fleet-foot roe that's tired with chasing,
562 Or like the froward infant stilled with dandling,
    He now obeys and now no more resisteth,
564   While she takes all she can, not all she listeth.

565 What wax so frozen but dissolves with temp'ring
And yields at last to every light impression?
567 Things out of hope are compassed oft with vent'ring,
568 Chiefly in love, whose leave exceeds commission.
569   Affection faints not like a pale-faced coward,
570   But then woos best when most his choice is froward.

---

550 *insulter* i.e. triumphant winner   551 *vulture* i.e. ravenous   555 *reek* i.e.
steam   557 *Planting oblivion* i.e. implanting blind disregard of conse-
quences   558 *wrack* wreck   562 *froward* fretful   564 *listeth* wishes   565
temp'ring heating   567 *out of* beyond; *compassed* accomplished; *vent'ring*
venturing   568 *leave . . . commission* i.e. liberties exceed permission
569 *Affection* passion   570 *when . . . froward* i.e. when the object of his
desire is most stubborn

When he did frown, O, had she then gave over,
Such nectar from his lips she had not sucked.
Foul words and frowns must not repel a lover. 573
What though the rose have prickles, yet 'tis plucked.
　　Were beauty under twenty locks kept fast,
　　Yet love breaks through and picks them all at last.

For pity now she can no more detain him;
The poor fool prays her that he may depart. 578
She is resolved no longer to restrain him;
Bids him farewell, and look well to her heart,
　　The which, by Cupid's bow she doth protest,
　　He carries thence incagèd in his breast.

'Sweet boy,' she says, 'this night I'll waste in sorrow, 583
For my sick heart commands mine eyes to watch. 584
Tell me, love's master, shall we meet to-morrow?
Say, shall we? shall we? wilt thou make the match?'
　　He tells her no; to-morrow he intends
　　To hunt the boar with certain of his friends.

'The boar!' quoth she; whereat a sudden pale, 589
Like lawn being spread upon the blushing rose,
Usurps her cheek; she trembles at his tale,
And on his neck her yoking arms she throws;
　　She sinketh down, still hanging by his neck,
　　He on her belly falls, she on her back.

573 *Foul* hostile　578 *fool* plaything　583 *waste* spend　584 *watch* remain
open　589 *pale* pallor

595 Now is she in the very lists of love,
 Her champion mounted for the hot encounter.
597 All is imaginary she doth prove,
598 He will not manage her, although he mount her;
599   That worse than Tantalus' is her annoy,
600   To clip Elysium and to lack her joy.

 Even so poor birds, deceived with painted grapes,
602 Do surfeit by the eye and pine the maw;
 Even so she languisheth in her mishaps
 As those poor birds that helpless berries saw.
605   The warm effects which she in him finds missing
   She seeks to kindle with continual kissing.

 But all in vain. Good Queen, it will not be!
608 She hath assayed as much as may be proved.
 Her pleading hath deserved a greater fee:
 She's Love, she loves, and yet she is not loved.
   'Fie, fie!' he says. 'You crush me; let me go!
   You have no reason to withhold me so.'

 'Thou hadst been gone,' quoth she, 'sweet boy, ere this,
 But that thou told'st me thou wouldst hunt the boar.
 O, be advised, thou know'st not what it is
 With javelin's point a churlish swine to gore,
617   Whose tushes never sheathed he whetteth still,
618   Like to a mortal butcher bent to kill.

---

595 *lists* field of combat   597 *prove* experience   598 *manage* ride   599
That . . . annoy i.e. so that her torment exceeds that of Tantalus (punished in
Hades by sight of unobtainable food and drink)   600 *clip* embrace;
Elysium pagan paradise (here Adonis)   602 *pine the maw* starve the stomach
605 *effects* symptoms   608 *assayed* tried; *proved* tried   617 *tushes* tusks
618 *mortal* deadly

'On his bow-back he hath a battle set
Of bristly pikes that ever threat his foes;
His eyes like glowworms shine when he doth fret;
His snout digs sepulchres where'er he goes;
    Being moved, he strikes whate'er is in his way,   623
    And whom he strikes his crooked tushes slay.

'His brawny sides, with hairy bristles armèd,
Are better proof than thy spear's point can enter;   626
His short thick neck cannot be easily harmèd;
Being ireful, on the lion he will venter.   628
    The thorny brambles and embracing bushes,
    As fearful of him, part; through whom he rushes.

'Alas, he naught esteems that face of thine,
To which Love's eyes pays tributary gazes;
Nor thy soft hands, sweet lips, and crystal eyne,   633
Whose full perfection all the world amazes;
    But having thee at vantage (wondrous dread!)   635
    Would root these beauties as he roots the mead.   636

'O, let him keep his loathsome cabin still: 637
Beauty hath naught to do with such foul fiends.   638
Come not within his danger by thy will: 639
They that thrive well take counsel of their friends.
    When thou didst name the boar, not to dissemble,
    I feared thy fortune, and my joints did tremble.

---

623 *moved* angered   626 *better proof* stronger armor   628 *venter* venture
633 *eyne* eyes   635 *vantage* an advantage   636 *root* root up   637 *cabin* i.e.
natural sty   638 *fiends* destroyers   639 *danger* i.e. zone of danger

'Didst thou not mark my face? Was it not white?
Saw'st thou not signs of fear lurk in mine eye?
645   Grew I not faint? and fell I not downright?
Within my bosom, whereon thou dost lie,
647   My boding heart pants, beats, and takes no rest,
     But, like an earthquake, shakes thee on my breast.

649   'For where Love reigns, disturbing Jealousy
Doth call himself Affection's sentinel,
651   Gives false alarms, suggesteth mutiny,
And in a peaceful hour doth cry "Kill, kill!"
653   Distemp'ring gentle Love in his desire,
     As air and water do abate the fire.

655   'This sour informer, this bate-breeding spy,
656   This canker that eats up Love's tender spring,
This carry-tale, dissentious Jealousy,
That sometime true news, sometime false doth bring,
     Knocks at my heart, and whispers in mine ear
     That if I love thee, I thy death should fear;

'And more than so, presenteth to mine eye
The picture of an angry-chafing boar,
Under whose sharp fangs on his back doth lie
An image like thyself, all stained with gore;
     Whose blood upon the fresh flowers being shed
     Doth make them droop with grief and hang the head.

---

645 *downright* without pause **647** *boding* foreboding **649** *Jealousy* apprehension **651** *suggesteth mutiny* incites violence **653** *Distemp'ring* reducing **655** *bate-breeding* strife-breeding **656** *canker* rose-worm; *spring* shoot

'What should I do, seeing thee so indeed,
That tremble at th' imagination?
The thought of it doth make my faint heart bleed,
And fear doth teach it divination.   670
   I prophesy thy death, my living sorrow,
   If thou encounter with the boar to-morrow.

'But if thou needs wilt hunt, be ruled by me;
Uncouple at the timorous flying hare,   674
Or at the fox which lives by subtlety,
Or at the roe which no encounter dare.
   Pursue these fearful creatures o'er the downs,   677
   And on thy well-breathed horse keep with thy hounds. 678

'And when thou hast on foot the purblind hare,   679
Mark the poor wretch, to overshoot his troubles,   680
How he outruns the wind, and with what care
He cranks and crosses with a thousand doubles.   682
   The many musits through the which he goes   683
   Are like a labyrinth to amaze his foes.   684

'Sometime he runs among a flock of sheep,
To make the cunning hounds mistake their smell,
And sometime where earth-delving conies keep,   687
To stop the loud pursuers in their yell;   688
   And sometime sorteth with a herd of deer.   689
   Danger deviseth shifts, wit waits on fear;   690

670 *divination* power to prophesy   674 *Uncouple at* loose your hound upon
677 *fearful* timid   678 *well-breathed* sound-winded; *keep* keep up   679 *on
foot* in chase; *purblind* dimsighted   680 *overshoot* run beyond   682 *cranks*
turns   683 *musits* gaps in a hedge or fence   684 *amaze* confuse   687 *conies*
rabbits   688 *yell* full cry   689 *sorteth* mingles   690 *shifts* ruses; *waits on*
goes with

'For there his smell with others being mingled,
The hot scent-snuffing hounds are driven to doubt,
Ceasing their clamorous cry till they have singled
694   With much ado the cold fault cleanly out.
      Then do they spend their mouths; echo replies,
      As if another chase were in the skies.

697   'By this, poor Wat, far off upon a hill,
Stands on his hinder legs with list'ning ear,
To hearken if his foes pursue him still.
Anon their loud alarums he doth hear,
      And now his grief may be comparèd well
702   To one sore sick that hears the passing bell.

'Then shalt thou see the dew-bedabbled wretch
704   Turn and return, indenting with the way.
705   Each envious brier his weary legs do scratch;
Each shadow makes him stop, each murmur stay;
      For misery is trodden on by many
      And, being low, never relieved by any.

'Lie quietly and hear a little more.
Nay, do not struggle, for thou shalt not rise.
To make thee hate the hunting of the boar,
Unlike myself thou hear'st me moralize,
      Applying this to that, and so to so;
      For love can comment upon every woe.

694 *cold fault* lost scent   697 *Wat* hare (popular term)   702 *passing* funeral
704 *indenting* zigzagging   705 *envious* malicious

'Where did I leave?' 'No matter where,' quoth he;
'Leave me, and then the story aptly ends.
The night is spent.' 'Why, what of that?' quoth she.
'I am,' quoth he, 'expected of my friends;
    And now 'tis dark, and going I shall fall.'
     'In night,' quoth she, 'desire sees best of all.

'But if thou fall, O, then imagine this:
The earth, in love with thee, thy footing trips,
And all is but to rob thee of a kiss.
Rich preys make true men thieves. So do thy lips   724
    Make modest Dian cloudy and forlorn,   725
    Lest she should steal a kiss and die forsworn.   726

'Now of this dark night I perceive the reason: 727
Cynthia for shame obscures her silver shine,   728
Till forging Nature be condemned of treason   729
For stealing moulds from heaven that were divine;
    Wherein she framed thee, in high heaven's despite,
    To shame the sun by day, and her by night.   732

'And therefore hath she bribed the Destinies
To cross the curious workmanship of Nature,   734
To mingle beauty with infirmities
And pure perfection with impure defeature,   736
    Making it subject to the tyranny
    Of mad mischances and much misery;

724 *preys* spoils   725 *Dian* Diana (chaste goddess of the moon)   726 *for-sworn* i.e. violating the oath of chastity   727 *of* for   728 *Cynthia* i.e. Diana   729 *forging* counterfeiting   732 *her* i.e. the moon   734 *cross* thwart; *curious* ingenious   736 *defeature* defect

'As burning fevers, agues pale and faint,
740 Life-poisoning pestilence, and frenzies wood,
741 The marrow-eating sickness whose attaint
Disorder breeds by heating of the blood,
743   Surfeits, imposthumes, grief, and damned despair
    Swear Nature's death for framing thee so fair.

745 'And not the least of all these maladies
But in one minute's fight brings beauty under.
747 Both favor, savor, hue, and qualities,
748 Whereat th' impartial gazer late did wonder,
    Are on the sudden wasted, thawed, and done,
    As mountain snow melts with the midday sun.

751 'Therefore, despite of fruitless chastity,
752 Love-lacking vestals, and self-loving nuns,
That on the earth would breed a scarcity
And barren dearth of daughters and of sons,
755   Be prodigal. The lamp that burns by night
    Dries up his oil to lend the world his light.

'What is thy body but a swallowing grave,
Seeming to bury that posterity
759 Which by the rights of time thou needs must have
If thou destroy them not in dark obscurity?
    If so, the world will hold thee in disdain,
762   Sith in thy pride so fair a hope is slain.

---

740 *wood* mad   741 *attaint* infection   743 *imposthumes* abscesses   745–46 *And . . . under* i.e. the least of these maladies subdues beauty in a minute 747 *favor* features   748 *impartial* just   751 *fruitless* sterile   752 *self-loving* i.e. intent upon their own salvation (?)   755 *prodigal* i.e. outgiving   759 *rights* claims   762 *Sith* since

'So in thyself thyself art made away,
A mischief worse than civil home-bred strife,
Or theirs whose desperate hands themselves do slay,
Or butcher sire that reaves his son of life.   766
   Foul cank'ring rust the hidden treasure frets,   767
   But gold that's put to use more gold begets.'

'Nay, then,' quoth Adon, 'you will fall again
Into your idle over-handled theme.   770
The kiss I gave you is bestowed in vain,
And all in vain you strive against the stream;
   For, by this black-faced night, desire's foul nurse,
   Your treatise makes me like you worse and worse.   774

'If love have lent you twenty thousand tongues,
And every tongue more moving than your own,
Bewitching like the wanton mermaid's songs,
Yet from mine ear the tempting tune is blown;
   For know, my heart stands armèd in mine ear   779
   And will not let a false sound enter there,

'Lest the deceiving harmony should run
Into the quiet closure of my breast;   782
And then my little heart were quite undone,
In his bedchamber to be barred of rest.
   No, lady, no; my heart longs not to groan,
   But soundly sleeps while now it sleeps alone.

766 *reaves* deprives   767 *cank'ring* eating (as does the canker-worm); *frets* erodes   770 *over-handled* threadbare   774 *treatise* discourse   779 *heart* i.e. inner resolution   782 *closure* enclosure

787   'What have you urged that I cannot reprove?
The path is smooth that leadeth on to danger.
789   I hate not love, but your device in love,
That lends embracements unto every stranger.
   You do it for increase. O strange excuse,
   When reason is the bawd to lust's abuse!

'Call it not love, for Love to heaven is fled
Since sweating Lust on earth unsurped his name;
795   Under whose simple semblance he hath fed
Upon fresh beauty, blotting it with blame;
797   Which the hot tyrant stains and soon bereaves,
    As caterpillars do the tender leaves.

'Love comforteth like sunshine after rain,
But Lust's effect is tempest after sun.
Love's gentle spring doth always fresh remain;
Lust's winter comes ere summer half be done.
   Love surfeits not, Lust like a glutton dies;
   Love is all truth, Lust full of forgèd lies.

'More I could tell, but more I dare not say:
806   The text is old, the orator too green.
807   Therefore in sadness now I will away.
808   My face is full of shame, my heart of teen;
   Mine ears, that to your wanton talk attended,
   Do burn themselves for having so offended.'

787 *reprove* refute   789 *device* i.e. sleights   795 *simple semblance* guileless aspect   797 *hot tyrant* i.e. lust; *bereaves* impairs, spoils   806 *green* unripe, inexperienced   807 *in sadness* in all seriousness   808 *teen* grief

With this he breaketh from the sweet embrace
Of those fair arms which bound him to her breast
And homeward through the dark laund runs apace; 813
Leaves Love upon her back, deeply distressed.
　　Look how a bright star shooteth from the sky,
　　So glides he in the night from Venus' eye;

Which after him she darts, as one on shore
Gazing upon a late-embarkèd friend
Till the wild waves will have him seen no more,
Whose ridges with the meeting clouds contend.
　　So did the merciless and pitchy night
　　Fold in the object that did feed her sight.

Whereat amazed, as one that unaware 823
Hath dropped a precious jewel in the flood,
Or stonished as night-wand'rers often are, 825
Their light blown out in some mistrustful wood, 826
　　Even so confounded in the dark she lay,
　　Having lost the fair discovery of her way.

And now she beats her heart, whereat it groans,
That all the neighbor caves, as seeming troubled,
Make verbal repetition of her moans.
Passion on passion deeply is redoubled: 832
　　'Ay me!' she cries, and twenty times, 'Woe, woe!'
　　And twenty echoes twenty times cry so.

813 *laund* i.e. grassy fields 823 *amazed* confused, at a loss 825 *stonished* dismayed 826 *mistrustful* mistrusted, feared 832 *Passion* lamentation; *redoubled* re-echoed

She, marking them, begins a wailing note
And sings extemporally a woeful ditty –
837 How love makes young men thrall, and old men dote;
How love is wise in folly, foolish-witty.
　　Her heavy anthem still concludes in woe,
　　And still the choir of echoes answer so.

Her song was tedious and outwore the night,
For lovers' hours are long, though seeming short.
If pleased themselves, others, they think, delight
In such-like circumstance, with such-like sport.
　　Their copious stories, oftentimes begun,
　　End without audience and are never done.

For who hath she to spend the night withal
848 But idle sounds resembling parasits,
Like shrill-tongued tapsters answering every call,
Soothing the humor of fantastic wits?
　　She says ' 'Tis so.' They answer all, ' 'Tis so,'
　　And would say after her if she said 'No.'

Lo, here the gentle lark, weary of rest,
854 From his moist cabinet mounts up on high
And wakes the morning, from whose silver breast
The sun ariseth in his majesty;
　　Who doth the world so gloriously behold
　　That cedar tops and hills seem burnished gold.

837 *thrall* captive　848 *parasits* parasites, attendants　854 *moist cabinet*
dewy cottage

Venus salutes him with this fair good-morrow:
'O thou clear god, and patron of all light,
From whom each lamp and shining star doth borrow
The beauteous influence that makes him bright,
    There lives a son that sucked an earthly mother
    May lend thee light, as thou dost lend to other.'

This said, she hasteth to a myrtle grove,
Musing the morning is so much o'erworn
And yet she hears no tidings of her love.
She hearkens for his hounds and for his horn.
    Anon she hears them chant it lustily,
    And all in haste she coasteth to the cry;   870

And as she runs, the bushes in the way
Some catch her by the neck, some kiss her face,
Some twind about her thigh to make her stay.   873
She wildly breaketh from their strict embrace,   874
    Like a milch doe whose swelling dugs do ache
    Hasting to feed her fawn hid in some brake.

By this, she hears the hounds are at a bay;   877
Whereat she starts, like one that spies an adder
Wreathed up in fatal folds just in his way,
The fear whereof doth make him shake and shudder.
    Even so the timorous yelping of the hounds
    Appals her senses and her spirit confounds.

---

870 *coasteth to* runs to head off   873 *twind* wind   874 *strict* tight   877 *at a bay* i.e. confronted by their quarry

For now she knows it is no gentle chase,
884 But the blunt boar, rough bear, or lion proud,
Because the cry remaineth in one place,
Where fearfully the dogs exclaim aloud.
887   Finding their enemy to be so curst,
888   They all strain court'sy who shall cope him first.

This dismal cry rings sadly in her ear,
890 Through which it enters to surprise her heart,
Who, overcome by doubt and bloodless fear,
892 With cold-pale weakness numbs each feeling part:
    Like soldiers when their captain once doth yield,
    They basely fly and dare not stay the field.

895 Thus stands she in a trembling ecstasy;
Till, cheering up her senses all dismayed,
897 She tells them 'tis a causeless fantasy,
And childish error that they are afraid;
    Bids them leave quaking, bids them fear no more;
    And with that word she spied the hunted boar,

Whose frothy mouth, bepainted all with red,
Like milk and blood being mingled both togither,
A second fear through all her sinews spread,
Which madly hurries her she knows not whither.
    This way she runs, and now she will no further,
    But back retires to rate the boar for murther.

---

884 *blunt* crude 887 *curst* fierce-tempered 888 *strain court'sy* i.e. are over-polite in yielding precedence; *cope* cope with 890 *surprise* attack 892 *feeling part* organ of sense 895 *ecstasy* fit 897 *causeless fantasy* baseless fancy

A thousand spleens bear her a thousand ways ;　　907
She treads the path that she untreads again ;
Her more than haste is mated with delays,　　909
Like the proceedings of a drunken brain,
　　Full of respects, yet naught at all respecting,　　911
　　In hand with all things, naught at all effecting.　　912

Here kennelled in a brake she finds a hound
And asks the weary caitiff for his master ;　　914
And there another licking of his wound,
'Gainst venomed sores the only sovereign plaster ;　　916
　　And here she meets another, sadly scowling,
　　To whom she speaks, and he replies with howling.

When he hath ceased his ill-resounding noise,
Another flap-mouthed mourner, black and grim,　　920
Against the welkin volleys out his voice.
Another and another answer him,
　　Clapping their proud tails to the ground below,
　　Shaking their scratched ears, bleeding as they go.

Look how the world's poor people are amazèd　　925
At apparitions, signs, and prodigies,
Whereon with fearful eyes they long have gazèd,
Infusing them with dreadful prophecies :　　928
　　So she at these sad signs draws up her breath
　　And, sighing it again, exclaims on Death.　　930

907 *spleens* emotional starts　909 *mated* overcome　911 *respects* designs
912 *In hand with* busy about　914 *caitiff* base wretch　916 *plaster* dressing
920 *flap-mouthed* i.e. with dangling lips of a hound　925 *amazèd* perplexed
928 *Infusing . . . prophecies* i.e. converting them into dreadful omens　930
exclaims on inveighs against

'Hard-favored tyrant, ugly, meagre, lean,
932 Hateful divorce of love!' – thus chides she Death –
933 'Grim-grinning ghost, earth's worm, what dost thou mean
 To stifle beauty and to steal his breath
  Who, when he lived, his breath and beauty set
  Gloss on the rose, smell to the violet?

'If he be dead – O no, it cannot be,
Seeing his beauty, thou shouldst strike at it!
O yes, it may! Thou hast no eyes to see,
940 But hatefully at randon dost thou hit.
  Thy mark is feeble age; but thy false dart
  Mistakes that aim and cleaves an infant's heart.

'Hadst thou but bid beware, then he had spoke,
944 And, hearing him, thy power had lost his power.
The Destinies will curse thee for this stroke.
They bid thee crop a weed; thou pluck'st a flower.
  Love's golden arrow at him should have fled,
948 And not Death's ebon dart to strike him dead.

'Dost thou drink tears, that thou provok'st such weeping?
950 What may a heavy groan advantage thee?
Why hast thou cast into eternal sleeping
Those eyes that taught all other eyes to see?
953 Now Nature cares not for thy mortal vigor,
  Since her best work is ruined with thy rigor.'

---

932 *divorce* terminator 933 *worm* i.e. canker, begetter of rot 940 *randon* random 944 *his* its 948 *ebon* ebony, black 950 *advantage* profit 953 *mortal vigor* deadly strength

Here overcome, as one full of despair,
She vailed her eyelids, who, like sluices, stopped   956
The crystal tide that from her two cheeks fair
In the sweet channel of her bosom dropped;
    But through the floodgates breaks the silver rain
    And with his strong course opens them again.

O, how her eyes and tears did lend and borrow,   961
Her eye seen in the tears, tears in her eye,
Both crystals, where they viewed each other's sorrow —   963
Sorrow that friendly sighs sought still to dry;
    But like a stormy day, now wind, now rain,
    Sighs dry her cheeks, tears make them wet again.

Variable passions throng her constant woe,
As striving who should best become her grief.   968
All entertained, each passion labors so   969
That every present sorrow seemeth chief,
    But none is best; then join they all together
    Like many clouds consulting for foul weather.   972

By this, far off she hears some huntsman halloa.
A nurse's song ne'er pleased her babe so well.
The dire imagination she did follow
This sound of hope doth labor to expel;
    For now reviving joy bids her rejoice
    And flatters her it is Adonis' voice.

---

956 *vailed* lowered; *who . . . stopped* which, like floodgates, dammed 961
lend and borrow i.e. reflect each other 963 *crystals* i.e. mirrors 968
striving who contending which 969 *entertained* admitted 972 *consulting
for* i.e. planning to produce

979 Whereat her tears began to turn their tide,
980 Being prisoned in her eye like pearls in glass;
Yet sometimes falls an orient drop beside,
982 Which her cheek melts, as scorning it should pass
　　To wash the foul face of the sluttish ground,
　　Who is but drunken when she seemeth drowned.

985 O hard-believing love, how strange it seems
Not to believe, and yet too credulous!
987 Thy weal and woe are both of them extremes;
Despair and hope makes thee ridiculous:
989 　The one doth flatter thee in thoughts unlikely,
990 　In likely thoughts the other kills thee quickly.

Now she unweaves the web that she hath wrought:
Adonis lives, and Death is not to blame;
993 It was not she that called him all to naught.
Now she adds honors to his hateful name:
995 　She clepes him king of graves, and grave for kings,
996 　Imperious supreme of all mortal things.

'No, no,' quoth she, 'sweet Death, I did but jest;
Yet pardon me I felt a kind of fear
When as I met the boar, that bloody beast
Which knows no pity but is still severe.
1001 　Then, gentle shadow (truth I must confess),
1002 　I railed on thee, fearing my love's decesse.

---

979 *turn their tide* ebb, subside　980 *like . . . glass* i.e. with the fixed quality of a pearl-shaped glass-bubble (?)　982 *melts* i.e. reduces to mere moisture　985 *hard-believing* i.e. stubborn, wrongheaded　987 *weal* gladness　989 *The one* i.e. hope; *thoughts unlikely* i.e. cheerful fancies　990 *likely thoughts* i.e. ominous probabilities　993 *all to naught* evil　995 *clepes* names　996 *Imperious supreme* imperial ruler　1001 *shadow* shade, spectre　1002 *decesse* decease

' 'Tis not my fault the boar provoked my tongue.
Be wreaked on him, invisible commander;   1004
'Tis he, foul creature, that hath done thee wrong.
I did but act; he's author of thy slander.
    Grief hath two tongues, and never woman yet
    Could rule them both without ten women's wit.'

Thus hoping that Adonis is alive,
Her rash suspect she doth extenuate;   1010
And that his beauty may the better thrive,
With Death she humbly doth insinuate;   1012
    Tells him of trophies, statues, tombs; and stories   1013
    His victories, his triumphs, and his glories.

'O Jove,' quoth she, 'how much a fool was I
To be of such a weak and silly mind
To wail his death who lives, and must not die
Till mutual overthrow of mortal kind!
    For he being dead, with him is beauty slain,
    And, beauty dead, black chaos comes again.

'Fie, fie, fond love, thou art as full of fear
As one with treasure laden hemmed with thieves.
Trifles, unwitnessèd with eye or ear,   1023
Thy coward heart with false bethinking grieves.'
    Even at this word she hears a merry horn,
    Whereat she leaps that was but late forlorn.

1004 *wreaked* revenged   1010 *suspect* suspicion   1012 *insinuate* ingratiate
herself   1013 *stories* narrates   1023 *unwitnessèd with* not perceived by

As falcons to the lure, away she flies.
The grass stoops not, she treads on it so light;
And in her haste unfortunately spies
The foul boar's conquest on her fair delight;
    Which seen, her eyes, as murd'red with the view,
1032   Like stars ashamed of day, themselves withdrew;

Or as the snail, whose tender horns being hit,
Shrinks backward in his shelly cave with pain,
And there, all smooth'red up, in shade doth sit,
Long after fearing to creep forth again;
    So at his bloody view her eyes are fled
    Into the deep-dark cabins of her head;

Where they resign their office and their light
To the disposing of her troubled brain;
1041   Who bids them still consort with ugly night
1042   And never wound the heart with looks again;
1043   Who, like a king perplexèd in his throne,
1044   By their suggestion gives a deadly groan,

Whereat each tributary subject quakes,
As when the wind, imprisoned in the ground,
Struggling for passage, earth's foundation shakes,
Which with cold terror doth men's minds confound.
1049   This mutiny each part doth so surprise
    That from their dark beds once more leap her eyes,

1032 *ashamed of* put to shame by   1041 *still consort* always dwell   1042 *looks* i.e. looking   1043 *Who* i.e. which; *perplexèd* tormented   1044 *suggestion* incitement   1049 *mutiny* attack

And, being opened, threw unwilling light
Upon the wide wound that the boar had trenched   1052
In his soft flank; whose wonted lily white
With purple tears that his wound wept was drenched.
   No flow'r was nigh, no grass, herb, leaf, or weed,
   But stole his blood and seemed with him to bleed.

This solemn sympathy poor Venus noteth.
Over one shoulder doth she hang her head.
Dumbly she passions, franticly she doteth: 1059
She thinks he could not die, he is not dead;
   Her voice is stopped, her joints forget to bow;
   Her eyes are mad that they have wept till now.   1062

Upon his hurt she looks so steadfastly
That her sight dazzling makes the wound seem three;   1064
And then she reprehends her mangling eye,
That makes more gashes where no breach should be.
   His face seems twain, each several limb is doubled;
   For oft the eye mistakes, the brain being troubled.

'My tongue cannot express my grief for one,
And yet,' quoth she, 'behold two Adons dead!
My sighs are blown away, my salt tears gone,
Mine eyes are turned to fire, my heart to lead.
   Heavy heart's lead, melt at mine eyes' red fire!
   So shall I die by drops of hot desire.

1052 *trenched* ripped   1059 *passions* grieves, displays emotion   1062 *mad*
frenzied; *till* i.e. before   1064 *dazzling* i.e. losing distinctness of vision

'Alas, poor world, what treasure hast thou lost!
What face remains alive that's worth the viewing?
Whose tongue is music now? What canst thou boast
1078   Of things long since, or any thing ensuing?
    The flowers are sweet, their colors fresh and trim;
    But true-sweet beauty lived and died with him.

'Bonnet nor veil henceforth no creature wear!
Nor sun nor wind will ever strive to kiss you.
1083   Having no fair to lose, you need not fear.
The sun doth scorn you, and the wind doth hiss you;
    But when Adonis lived, sun and sharp air
    Lurked like two thieves, to rob him of his fair;

'And therefore would he put his bonnet on,
Under whose brim the gaudy sun would peep;
The wind would blow it off, and, being gone,
Play with his locks, then would Adonis weep;
    And straight, in pity of his tender years,
    They both would strive who first should dry his tears.

'To see his face the lion walked along
1094   Behind some hedge, because he would not fear him.
To recreate himself when he hath song,
The tiger would be tame, and gently hear him.
    If he had spoke, the wolf would leave his prey
    And never fright the silly lamb that day.

1078 *long since* i.e. far in the past   1083 *fair* beauty   1094 *fear* frighten

'When he beheld his shadow in the brook,
The fishes spread on it their golden gills.
When he was by, the birds such pleasure took
That some would sing, some other in their bills
    Would bring him mulberries and ripe-red cherries:
    He fed them with his sight, they him with berries.

'But this foul, grim, and urchin-snouted boar,   1105
Whose downward eye still looketh for a grave,
Ne'er saw the beauteous livery that he wore: 1107
Witness the entertainment that he gave.   1108
    If he did see his face, why then I know
    He thought to kiss him, and hath killed him so.

' 'Tis true, 'tis true! thus was Adonis slain:
He ran upon the boar with his sharp spear,
Who did not whet his teeth at him again,
But by a kiss thought to persuade him there;
    And nuzzling in his flank, the loving swine
    Sheathed unaware the tusk in his soft groin.

'Had I been toothed like him, I must confess,
With kissing him I should have killed him first;
But he is dead, and never did he bless
My youth with his – the more am I accurst.'   1120
    With this, she falleth in the place she stood
    And stains her face with his congealèd blood.

1105 *urchin-snouted* hedgehog-snouted, i.e. rooting   1107 *livery* i.e. outsides, appearance   1108 *entertainment* treatment

She looks upon his lips, and they are pale;
She takes him by the hand, and that is cold;
She whispers in his ears a heavy tale,
As if they heard the woeful words she told;
  She lifts the coffer-lids that close his eyes,
  Where, lo, two lamps burnt out in darkness lies;

Two glasses, where herself herself beheld
A thousand times, and now no more reflect,
Their virtue lost wherein they late excelled,
And every beauty robbed of his effect.
1133 'Wonder of time,' quoth she, 'this is my spite,
  That, thou being dead, the day should yet be light.

'Since thou art dead, lo, here I prophesy
Sorrow on love hereafter shall attend.
1137 It shall be waited on with jealousy,
Find sweet beginning, but unsavory end,
  Ne'er settled equally, but high or low,
  That all love's pleasure shall not match his woe.

'It shall be fickle, false, and full of fraud,
1142 Bud and be blasted in a breathing while,
1143 The bottom poison, and the top o'erstrawed
With sweets that shall the truest sight beguile.
  The strongest body shall it make most weak,
  Strike the wise dumb, and teach the fool to speak.

1133 *spite* torment 1137 *jealousy* apprehension of evil 1142 *breathing while* space of a breath 1143 *o'erstrawed* overstrewn

'It shall be sparing, and too full of riot,
Teaching decrepit age to tread the measures;
The staring ruffian shall it keep in quiet,   1149
Pluck down the rich, enrich the poor with treasures;
   It shall be raging mad and silly mild,
   Make the young old, the old become a child.

'It shall suspect where is no cause of fear;
It shall not fear where it should most mistrust;
It shall be merciful, and too severe,
And most deceiving when it seems most just;
   Perverse it shall be where it shows most toward,   1157
   Put fear to valor, courage to the coward.

'It shall be cause of war and dire events
And set dissension 'twixt the son and sire,
Subject and servile to all discontents,
As dry combustious matter is to fire.
   Sith in his prime death doth my love destroy,
   They that love best their loves shall not enjoy.'

By this, the boy that by her side lay killed
Was melted like a vapor from her sight,
And in his blood, that on the ground lay spilled,
A purple flower sprung up, check'red with white,   1168
   Resembling well his pale cheeks and the blood
   Which in round drops upon their whiteness stood.

1149 *staring* glaring, threatening   1157 *toward* tractable   1168 *purple
flower* i.e. the anemone (cf. Ovid, *Metamorphoses*, x, 731–39)

She bows her head the new-sprung flower to smell,
Comparing it to her Adonis' breath,
And says within her bosom it shall dwell,
Since he himself is reft from her by death;
 She crops the stalk, and in the breach appears
 Green-dropping sap, which she compares to tears.

1177   'Poor flow'r,' quoth she, 'this was thy father's guise –
Sweet issue of a more sweet-smelling sire –
For every little grief to wet his eyes.
To grow unto himself was his desire,
 And so 'tis thine; but know, it is as good
 To wither in my breast as in his blood.

'Here was thy father's bed, here in my breast;
Thou art the next of blood, and 'tis thy right.
Lo, in this hollow cradle take thy rest;
My throbbing heart shall rock thee day and night.
 There shall not be one minute in an hour
 Wherein I will not kiss my sweet love's flow'r.'

Thus weary of the world, away she hies
And yokes her silver doves, by whose swift aid
Their mistress, mounted, through the empty skies
In her light chariot quickly is conveyed,
1193   Holding their course to Paphos, where their queen
 Means to immure herself and not be seen.

FINIS

1177 *guise* i.e. way, manner   1193 *Paphos* (the abode of Venus in Cyprus)

THE RAPE OF LUCRECE

TO THE RIGHT HONORABLE

HENRY WRIOTHESLEY

EARL OF SOUTHAMPTON,
AND BARON OF TITCHFIELD

The love I dedicate to your Lordship is without end; whereof this pamphlet without beginning is but a superfluous moiety. The warrant I have of your honorable disposition, not the worth of my untutored lines, makes it assured of acceptance. What I have done is yours; what I have to do is yours; being part in all I have, devoted yours. Were my worth greater, my duty would show greater; meantime, as it is, it is bound to your Lordship, to whom I wish long life still lengthened with all happiness.

Your Lordship's in all duty,
WILLIAM SHAKESPEARE

Ded., **6** *without beginning* (often explained as signifying that the story begins *in medias res*, but perhaps only a vague term of deprecation, i.e. 'maimed,' 'imperfect') **7** *superfluous moiety* i.e. uncontained portion, spillover; *warrant* assurance

THE RAPE OF LUCRECE

THE ARGUMENT

Lucius Tarquinius (for his excessive pride surnamed
Superbus), after he had caused his own father-in-law
Servius Tullius to be cruelly murdered, and, contrary to
the Roman laws and customs, not requiring or staying for
the people's suffrages, had possessed himself of the king-
dom, went, accompanied with his sons and other noblemen of Rome, to besiege Ardea; during which siege the
principal men of the army meeting one evening at the tent
of Sextus Tarquinius, the King's son, in their discourses
after supper every one commended the virtues of his own
wife; among whom Collatinus extolled the incomparable
chastity of his wife Lucretia. In that pleasant humor they
all posted to Rome; and intending by their secret and
sudden arrival to make trial of that which every one had
before avouched, only Collatinus finds his wife (though it
were late in the night) spinning amongst her maids; the
other ladies were all found dancing and revelling, or in
several disports. Whereupon the noblemen yielded Collatinus the victory, and his wife the fame. At that time
Sextus Tarquinius being inflamed with Lucrece' beauty, 20
yet smothering his passions for the present, departed with
the rest back to the camp; from whence he shortly after
privily withdrew himself, and was (according to his
estate) royally entertained and lodged by Lucrece at
Collatium. The same night he treacherously stealeth into

her chamber, violently ravished her, and early in the morning speedeth away. Lucrece, in this lamentable plight, hastily dispatcheth messengers, one to Rome for her father, another to the camp for Collatine. They came, the one accompanied with Junius Brutus, the other with Publius Valerius; and finding Lucrece attired in mourning habit, demanded the cause of her sorrow. She, first taking an oath of them for her revenge, revealed the actor and whole manner of his dealing, and withal suddenly stabbed herself. Which done, with one consent they all vowed to root out the whole hated family of the Tarquins; and bearing the dead body to Rome, Brutus acquainted the people with the doer and manner of the vile deed, with a bitter invective against the tyranny of the 40 King; wherewith the people were so moved that with one consent and a general acclamation the Tarquins were all exiled, and the state government changed from kings to consuls.

*

1   From the besiegèd Ardea all in post,
2   Borne by the trustless wings of false desire,
     Lust-breathèd Tarquin leaves the Roman host
4   And to Collatium bears the lightless fire
     Which, in pale embers hid, lurks to aspire
         And girdle with embracing flames the waist
         Of Collatine's fair love, Lucrece the chaste.

1 *all in post* post-haste   2 *trustless* treacherous   4 *lightless* i.e. smouldering

Haply that name of 'chaste' unhap'ly set 8
This bateless edge on his keen appetite; 9
When Collatine unwisely did not let 10
To praise the clear unmatchèd red and white
Which triumphed in that sky of his delight, 12
    Where mortal stars, as bright as heaven's beauties, 13
    With pure aspects did him peculiar duties. 14

For he the night before, in Tarquin's tent,
Unlocked the treasure of his happy state:
What priceless wealth the heavens had him lent
In the possession of his beauteous mate;
Reck'ning his fortune at such high proud rate
    That kings might be espousèd to more fame,
    But king nor peer to such a peerless dame.

O happiness enjoyed but of a few, 22
And, if possessed, as soon decayed and done 23
As is the morning's silver-melting dew
Against the golden splendor of the sun! 25
An expired date, cancelled ere well begun. 26
    Honor and beauty, in the owner's arms,
    Are weakly fortressed from a world of harms.

Beauty itself doth of itself persuade 29
The eyes of men without an orator. 30
What needeth then apologies be made 31
To set forth that which is so singular? 32
Or why is Collatine the publisher 33
    Of that rich jewel he should keep unknown
    From thievish ears, because it is his own?

8 *Haply* perchance 9 *bateless* unabated, sharp 10 *let* forbear 12 *sky* i.e. the face of Lucrece 13 *mortal stars* i.e. the eyes of Lucrece 14 *aspects* (1) gazes, (2) astrological portents; *peculiar duties* i.e. duties reserved for him 22 *of* by 23 *done* done with 25 *Against* i.e. in face of 26 *date* term 29 *of* by 30 *orator* pleader 31 *apologies* justifications 32 *singular* unique 33 *publisher* advertiser

Perchance his boast of Lucrece' sov'reignty
37 Suggested this proud issue of a king;
For by our ears our hearts oft tainted be.
Perchance that envy of so rich a thing
40 Braving compare, disdainfully did sting
His high-pitched thoughts that meaner men should vaunt
42 That golden hap which their superiors want.

But some untimely thought did instigate
44 His all too timeless speed, if none of those.
45 His honor, his affairs, his friends, his state,
Neglected all, with swift intent he goes
47 To quench the coal which in his liver glows.
48 O rash false heat, wrapped in repentant cold,
49 Thy hasty spring still blasts and ne'er grows old!

When at Collatium this false lord arrivèd,
Well was he welcomed by the Roman dame,
Within whose face Beauty and Virtue strivèd
53 Which of them both should underprop her fame.
When Virtue bragged, Beauty would blush for shame;
When Beauty boasted blushes, in despite
Virtue would stain that o'er with silver white.

57 But Beauty, in that white entitulèd,
58 From Venus' doves doth challenge that fair field.
Then Virtue claims from Beauty Beauty's red,
60 Which Virtue gave the Golden Age to gild
Their silver cheeks, and called it then their shield,
Teaching them thus to use it in the fight,
63 When shame assailed, the red should fence the white.

---

37 *Suggested* prompted; *issue* offspring 40 *Braving compare* defying comparisons 42 *hap* luck 44 *timeless* untimely 45 *state* i.e. royal status 47 *liver* (supposed seat of sexual desire) 48 *wrapped in* i.e. attended by 49 *blasts* is blasted 53 *underprop* bear up 57 *entitulèd* having a claim 58 *field* (1) field of combat, (2) armorial ground 60 *gild* i.e. cover with a blush of modesty 63 *fence* shield

THE RAPE OF LUCRECE

This heraldry in Lucrece' face was seen,
Argued by Beauty's red and Virtue's white.   65
Of either's color was the other queen,
Proving from world's minority their right.   67
Yet their ambition makes them still to fight,
   The sovereignty of either being so great   69
   That oft they interchange each other's seat.

This silent war of lilies and of roses
Which Tarquin viewed in her fair face's field,
In their pure ranks his traitor eye encloses;   73
Where, lest between them both it should be killed,
The coward captive vanquishèd doth yield
   To those two armies that would let him go
   Rather than triumph in so false a foe.

Now thinks he that her husband's shallow tongue,
The niggard prodigal that praised her so,
In that high task hath done her beauty wrong,
Which far exceeds his barren skill to show.   81
Therefore that praise which Collatine doth owe
   Enchanted Tarquin answers with surmise,   83
   In silent wonder of still-gazing eyes.

This earthly saint, adorèd by this devil,
Little suspecteth the false worshipper;
For unstained thoughts do seldom dream on evil;
Birds never limed no secret bushes fear.   88
So guiltless she securely gives good cheer   89
   And reverend welcome to her princely guest,
   Whose inward ill no outward harm expressed;

65 *Argued* disputed   67 *minority* youth, i.e. the Golden Age   69 *sovereignty*
natural superiority   73 *encloses* overwhelms   81 *show* i.e. do justice to   83
surmise i.e. mounting speculation   88 *limed* snared with birdlime   89
securely overconfidently

92   For that he colored with his high estate,
      Hiding base sin in pleats of majesty;
94   That nothing in him seemed inordinate,
      Save something too much wonder of his eye,
      Which, having all, all could not satisfy;
97   But, poorly rich, so wanteth in his store
        That, cloyed with much, he pineth still for more.

99   But she, that never coped with stranger eyes,
100   Could pick no meaning from their parling looks,
      Nor read the subtle-shining secrecies
102   Writ in the glassy margents of such books.
      She touched no unknown baits, nor feared no hooks;
104   Nor could she moralize his wanton sight,
105   More than his eyes were opened to the light.

      He stories to her ears her husband's fame,
      Won in the fields of fruitful Italy;
      And decks with praises Collatine's high name,
      Made glorious by his manly chivalry,
110   With bruisèd arms and wreaths of victory.
111   Her joy with heaved-up hand she doth express,
        And wordless so greets heaven for his success.

      Far from the purpose of his coming thither
      He makes excuses for his being there.
      No cloudy show of stormy blust'ring weather
116   Doth yet in his fair welkin once appear,
      Till sable Night, mother of dread and fear,
        Upon the world dim darkness doth display
        And in her vaulty prison stows the day.

---

92 *that he colored* i.e. the harmfulness he disguised   94 *That* so that   97 *store* abundance   99 *stranger eyes* eyes of a stranger   100 *parling* speaking 102 *glassy margents* mirroring margins   104 *moralize* interpret; *sight* glance 105 *than* than that   110 *bruisèd arms* battered armor   111 *heaved-up* upreared   116 *welkin* sky

For then is Tarquin brought unto his bed,
Intending weariness with heavy sprite;   121
For, after supper, long he questionèd   122
With modest Lucrece, and wore out the night.
Now leaden slumber with live's strength doth fight,   124
   And every one to rest themselves betake,
     Save thieves, and cares, and troubled minds that wake.   126

As one of which doth Tarquin lie revolving
The sundry dangers of his will's obtaining;
Yet ever to obtain his will resolving,
Though weak-built hopes persuade him to abstaining.   130
Despair to gain doth traffic oft for gaining;   131
   And when great treasure is the meed proposèd,   132
     Though death be adjunct, there's no death supposèd.   133

Those that much covet are with gain so fond   134
That what they have not, that which they possess,   135
They scatter and unloose it from their bond,   136
And so, by hoping more, they have but less;
Or, gaining more, the profit of excess
   Is but to surfeit, and such griefs sustain
     That they prove bankrout in this poor rich gain.   140

The aim of all is but to nurse the life
With honor, wealth, and ease in waning age;
And in this aim there is such thwarting strife   143
That one for all, or all for one we gage: 144
As life for honor in fell battle's rage;
   Honor for wealth; and oft that wealth doth cost
     The death of all, and all together lost;

---

121 *Intending* pretending; *sprite* spirit 122 *questionèd* discoursed 124
live's life's 126 *wake* keep watch 130 *weak-built hopes* i.e. small hope of
true felicity 131 *traffic* barter 132 *meed proposèd* i.e. reward in view 133
supposèd i.e. taken into consideration 134 *fond* infatuated 135 *what* for
what 136 *bond* i.e. possession 140 *bankrout* bankrupt 143 *And* but
144 *gage* stake

So that in vent'ring ill we leave to be
149 The things we are for that which we expect;
And this ambitious foul infirmity,
151 In having much, torments us with defect
152 Of that we have: so then we do neglect
The thing we have; and, all for want of wit,
Make something nothing by augmenting it.

Such hazard now must doting Tarquin make,
Pawning his honor to obtain his lust;
157 And for himself himself he must forsake.
Then where is truth, if there be no self-trust?
When shall he think to find a stranger just
160 When he himself himself confounds, betrays
To sland'rous tongues and wretched hateful days?

Now stole upon the time the dead of night,
When heavy sleep had closed up mortal eyes.
164 No comfortable star did lend his light,
No noise but owls' and wolves' death-boding cries.
Now serves the season that they may surprise
The silly lambs. Pure thoughts are dead and still,
While lust and murder wakes to stain and kill.

And now this lustful lord leapt from his bed,
Throwing his mantle rudely o'er his arm;
Is madly tossed between desire and dread:
Th' one sweetly flatters, th' other feareth harm;
But honest fear, bewitched with lust's foul charm,
Doth too too oft betake him to retire,
Beaten away by brainsick rude desire.

---

149 *expect* i.e. hope to be 151 *defect* i.e. the inadequacy 152 *neglect*
disregard 157 *himself himself* i.e. his physical self his true self 160
confounds ruins 164 *comfortable* comforting, propitious

His falchion on a flint he softly smiteth, 176
That from the cold stone sparks of fire do fly;
Whereat a waxen torch forthwith he lighteth,
Which must be lodestar to his lustful eye;
And to the flame thus speaks advisedly: 180
   'As from this cold flint I enforced this fire,
   So Lucrece must I force to my desire.'

Here pale with fear he doth premeditate
The dangers of his loathsome enterprise,
And in his inward mind he doth debate
What following sorrow may on this arise;
Then looking scornfully, he doth despise
   His naked armor of still-slaughterèd lust 188
   And justly thus controls his thoughts unjust:

'Fair torch, burn out thy light, and lend it not
To darken her whose light excelleth thine;
And die, unhallowed thoughts, before you blot
With your uncleanness that which is divine.
Offer pure incense to so pure a shrine.
   Let fair humanity abhor the deed
   That spots and stains love's modest snow-white weed. 196

'O shame to knighthood and to shining arms!
O foul dishonor to my household's grave! 198
O impious act including all foul harms!
A martial man to be soft fancy's slave!
True valor still a true respect should have; 201
   Then my digression is so vile, so base,
   That it will live engraven in my face.

176 *falchion* curved sword 180 *advisedly* deliberately 188 *His . . . lust*
i.e. his transient physical potency 196 *weed* garment 198 *grave* memorial
tomb 201 *respect* veneration

'Yea, though I die, the scandal will survive
205   And be an eyesore in my golden coat.
206   Some loathsome dash the herald will contrive
207   To cipher me how fondly I did dote;
      That my posterity, shamed with the note,
        Shall curse my bones, and hold it for no sin
        To wish that I their father had not been.

'What win I if I gain the thing I seek?
A dream, a breath, a froth of fleeting joy.
Who buys a minute's mirth to wail a week?
214   Or sells eternity to get a toy?
For one sweet grape who will the vine destroy?
      Or what fond beggar, but to touch the crown,
      Would with the sceptre straight be stroken down?

'If Collatinus dream of my intent,
Will he not wake, and in a desp'rate rage
Post hither this vile purpose to prevent?
221   This siege that hath engirt his marriage,
This blur to youth, this sorrow to the sage,
      This dying virtue, this surviving shame,
224   Whose crime will bear an ever-during blame?

'O, what excuse can my invention make
When thou shalt charge me with so black a deed?
Will not my tongue be mute, my frail joints shake,
Mine eyes forgo their light, my false heart bleed?
The guilt being great, the fear doth still exceed;
      And extreme fear can neither fight nor fly,
      But coward-like with trembling terror die.

---

205 *coat* coat of arms   206 *dash* bar, armorial abatement   207 *cipher* signal   214 *toy* trifle   221 *engirt* encroached upon   224 *ever-during* ever-enduring

'Had Collatinus killed my son or sire,
Or lain in ambush to betray my life,
Or were he not my dear friend, this desire
Might have excuse to work upon his wife,
As in revenge or quittal of such strife;   236
   But as he is my kinsman, my dear friend,
   The shame and fault finds no excuse nor end.

'Shameful it is. Ay, if the fact be known.
Hateful it is. There is no hate in loving.
I'll beg her love. But she is not her own.
The worst is but denial and reproving.
My will is strong, past reason's weak removing.   243
   Who fears a sentence or an old man's saw   244
   Shall by a painted cloth be kept in awe.'   245

Thus graceless holds he disputation
'Tween frozen conscience and hot-burning will,
And with good thoughts makes dispensation,   248
Urging the worser sense for vantage still;   249
Which in a moment doth confound and kill
   All pure effects, and doth so far proceed   251
   That what is vile shows like a virtuous deed.

Quoth he, 'She took me kindly by the hand
And gazed for tidings in my eager eyes,
Fearing some hard news from the warlike band
Where her belovèd Collatinus lies.
O, how her fear did make her color rise!
   First red as roses that on lawn we lay,
   Then white as lawn, the roses took away.

---

236 *quittal* requital   243 *removing* dissuasion   244 *sentence* moral maxim
245 *painted cloth* hanging painted with biblical or moral texts and illustra-
tions   248 *makes dispensation* dispenses   249 *vantage* advantage   251
effects impulses

'And how her hand, in my hand being locked,
Forced it to tremble with her loyal fear!
Which struck her sad, and then it faster rocked
Until her husband's welfare she did hear;
Whereat she smilèd with so sweet a cheer
265   That, had Narcissus seen her as she stood,
    Self-love had never drowned him in the flood.

267 'Why hunt I then for color or excuses?
    All orators are dumb when beauty pleadeth;
269 Poor wretches have remorse in poor abuses;
270 Love thrives not in the heart that shadows dreadeth.
271 Affection is my captain, and he leadeth;
    And when his gaudy banner is displayed,
273   The coward fights and will not be dismayed.

  'Then childish fear avaunt, debating die!
275 Respect and reason wait on wrinkled age!
276 My heart shall never countermand mine eye.
277 Sad pause and deep regard beseems the sage;
278 My part is youth, and beats these from the stage.
    Desire my pilot is, beauty my prize;
    Then who fears sinking where such treasure lies?'

---

265 *Narcissus* in classical myth, the youth who fell in love with his own image reflected in water, and was transformed into the narcissus 267 *color* disguising appearance 269 *Poor ... abuses* i.e. only the petty in their petty transgressions feel compunction 270 *shadows* i.e. the immaterial obstacles of conscience 271 *Affection* passion 273 *The coward* i.e. even the coward 275 *Respect* circumspection; *wait on* go with, attend 276 *countermand* run counter to 277 *Sad* serious 278 *stage* platform of action or disputation

As corn o'ergrown by weeds, so heedful fear   281
Is almost choked by unresisted lust.
Away he steals with open list'ning ear,
Full of foul hope and full of fond mistrust;
Both which, as servitors to the unjust,
    So cross him with their opposite persuasion   286
    That now he vows a league, and now invasion.   287

Within his thought her heavenly image sits,
And in the selfsame seat sits Collatine.
That eye which looks on her confounds his wits;
That eye which him beholds, as more divine,
Unto a view so false will not incline;
    But with a pure appeal seeks to the heart,   293
    Which once corrupted takes the worser part;

And therein heartens up his servile powers,   295
Who, flatt'red by their leader's jocund show,   296
Stuff up his lust, as minutes fill up hours;
And as their captain, so their pride doth grow,   298
Paying more slavish tribute than they owe.
    By reprobate desire thus madly led,
    The Roman lord marcheth to Lucrece' bed.

The locks between her chamber and his will,
Each one by him enforced retires his ward;   303
But, as they open, they all rate his ill,   304
Which drives the creeping thief to some regard.   305
The threshold grates the door to have him heard;
    Night-wand'ring weasels shriek to see him there;   307
    They fright him, yet he still pursues his fear.

---

281 *corn* grain 286 *cross* thwart 287 *league* i.e. treaty of non-aggression
293 *seeks to* seeks out, applies to 295 *servile powers* i.e. physical capacities
296 *Who* which 298 *as their captain* i.e. like their captain's (the heart's)
303 *his ward* (1) its locking bolt, (2) its posture of defense 304 *rate his ill*
scold his wickedness 305 *regard* caution 307 *weasels* i.e. domestic rat-
catchers (themselves furtive but startled by the furtive Tarquin)

As each unwilling portal yields him way,
Through little vents and crannies of the place
The wind wars with his torch to make him stay,
And blows the smoke of it into his face,
313 Extinguishing his conduct in this case;
    But his hot heart, which fond desire doth scorch,
    Puffs forth another wind that fires the torch;

316 And being lighted, by the light he spies
Lucretia's glove, wherein her needle sticks.
He takes it from the rushes where it lies,
And griping it, the needle his finger pricks,
As who should say, 'This glove to wanton tricks
321   Is not inured. Return again in haste –
    Thou seest our mistress' ornaments are chaste.'

323 But all these poor forbiddings could not stay him;
324 He in the worst sense consters their denial:
The doors, the wind, the glove, that did delay him,
326 He takes for accidental things of trial;
327 Or as those bars which stop the hourly dial,
328   Who with a ling'ring stay his course doth let
    Till every minute pays the hour his debt.

'So, so,' quoth he, 'these lets attend the time,
Like little frosts that sometime threat the spring
To add a more rejoicing to the prime
333 And give the sneapèd birds more cause to sing.
334 Pain pays the income of each precious thing:
    Huge rocks, high winds, strong pirates, shelves and sands,
    The merchant fears ere rich at home he lands.'

---

313 *conduct* conductor, i.e. the torch   316 *lighted* i.e. relighted   321 *inured* brazened   323 *stay* restrain   324 *consters* construes   326 *accidental . . . trial* i.e. morally insignificant tests of resolution   327 *bars . . . dial* the sixty check-points on the face of a clock   328 *Who* which; *his* its; *let* stop   333 *sneapèd* frost-nipped   334 *income* gain

Now is he come unto the chamber door
That shuts him from the heaven of his thought,
Which with a yielding latch, and with no more,
Hath barred him from the blessèd thing he sought.
So from himself impiety hath wrought   341
   That for his prey to pray he doth begin,
   As if the heavens should countenance his sin.

But in the midst of his unfruitful prayer,
Having solicited th' eternal power
That his foul thoughts might compass his fair fair,   346
And they would stand auspicious to the hour,
Even there he starts. Quoth he, 'I must deflow'r.
   The powers to whom I pray abhor this fact;
   How can they then assist me in the act?

'Then Love and Fortune be my gods, my guide:
My will is backed with resolution.
Thoughts are but dreams till their effects be tried;
The blackest sin is cleared with absolution;
Against love's fire fear's frost hath dissolution.
   The eye of heaven is out, and misty night
   Covers the shame that follows sweet delight.'

This said, his guilty hand plucked up the latch,
And with his knee the door he opens wide.
The dove sleeps fast that this night owl will catch.   360
Thus treason works ere traitors be espied.
Who sees the lurking serpent steps aside;
   But she, sound sleeping, fearing no such thing,
   Lies at the mercy of his mortal sting.

341 *wrought* i.e. wrought him   **346** *compass his fair fair* possess his virtuous fair one

Into the chamber wickedly he stalks
And gazeth on her yet unstainèd bed.
The curtains being close, about he walks,
Rolling his greedy eyeballs in his head.
By their high treason is his heart misled,
    Which gives the watchword to his hand full soon
    To draw the cloud that hides the silver moon.

Look, as the fair and fiery-pointed sun,
373 Rushing from forth a cloud, bereaves our sight,
Even so, the curtain drawn, his eyes begun
To wink, being blinded with a greater light;
Whether it is that she reflects so bright
377   That dazzleth them, or else some shame supposèd;
    But blind they are, and keep themselves enclosèd.

O, had they in that darksome prison died,
380 Then had they seen the period of their ill;
Then Collatine again, by Lucrece' side,
382 In his clear bed might have reposèd still.
But they must ope, this blessèd league to kill,
    And holy-thoughted Lucrece to their sight
    Must sell her joy, her life, her world's delight.

Her lily hand her rosy cheek lies under,
387 Coz'ning the pillow of a lawful kiss;
Who, therefore angry, seems to part in sunder,
389 Swelling on either side to want his bliss;
Between whose hills her head entombèd is;
    Where like a virtuous monument she lies,
    To be admired of lewd unhallowed eyes.

373 *bereaves* takes away   377 *supposèd* felt, apprehended   380 *period* end;
ill evil   382 *clear* innocent   387 *Coz'ning* cheating   389 *want* lack

THE RAPE OF LUCRECE

Without the bed her other fair hand was,
On the green coverlet; whose perfect white
Showed like an April daisy on the grass,
With pearly sweat resembling dew of night.
Her eyes, like marigolds, had sheathed their light,
    And canopied in darkness sweetly lay
    Till they might open to adorn the day.

Her hair like golden threads played with her breath –
O modest wantons, wanton modesty!
Showing life's triumph in the map of death,   402
And death's dim look in life's mortality.   403
Each in her sleep themselves so beautify
    As if between them twain there were no strife,
    But that life lived in death, and death in life.

Her breasts like ivory globes circled with blue,
A pair of maiden worlds unconquerèd,
Save of their lord no bearing yoke they knew,
And him by oath they truly honorèd.   410
These worlds in Tarquin new ambition bred,
    Who like a foul usurper went about
    From this fair throne to heave the owner out.

What could he see but mightily he noted?
What did he note but strongly he desirèd?
What he beheld, on that he firmly doted,
And in his will his willful eye he tirèd.   417
With more than admiration he admirèd
    Her azure veins, her alablaster skin,
    Her coral lips, her snow-white dimpled chin.

402 *map* image 403 *life's mortality* i.e. sleep 410 *by oath* i.e. in accordance
with the marriage vow 417 *will* lust

As the grim lion fawneth o'er his prey,
Sharp hunger by the conquest satisfied,
So o'er this sleeping soul doth Tarquin stay,
His rage of lust by gazing qualified ;
Slacked, not suppressed ; for, standing by her side,
426   His eye, which late this mutiny restrains,
        Unto a greater uproar tempts his veins ;

428 And they, like straggling slaves for pillage fighting,
Obdurate vassals fell exploits effecting,
In bloody death and ravishment delighting,
Nor children's tears nor mothers' groans respecting,
432 Swell in their pride, the onset still expecting.
        Anon his beating heart, alarum striking,
        Gives the hot charge and bids them do their liking.

His drumming heart cheers up his burning eye,
His eye commends the leading to his hand ;
His hand, as proud of such a dignity,
Smoking with pride, marched on to make his stand
On her bare breast, the heart of all her land ;
440   Whose ranks of blue veins, as his hand did scale,
        Left their round turrets destitute and pale.

442 They, must'ring to the quiet cabinet
Where their dear governess and lady lies,
Do tell her she is dreadfully beset
And fright her with confusion of their cries.
She, much amazed, breaks ope her locked-up eyes,
        Who, peeping forth this tumult to behold,
448   Are by his flaming torch dimmed and controlled.

426 *late* i.e. a moment before; *mutiny* i.e. rebellion of the blood, lust
428 *straggling* i.e. not in military order   432 *pride* lust   440 *scale* success-
fully mount (continuing the military imagery)   442 *must'ring* gathering;
cabinet the heart, where veins presumably would muster (?), or the brain,
where consciousness resides (?)   448 *controlled* overpowered

Imagine her as one in dead of night,
From forth dull sleep by dreadful fancy waking,
That thinks she hath beheld some ghastly sprite,
Whose grim aspect sets every joint a-shaking.
What terror 'tis! but she, in worser taking,   453
   From sleep disturbèd, heedfully doth view
   The sight which makes supposèd terror true.

Wrapped and confounded in a thousand fears,
Like to a new-killed bird she trembling lies.
She dares not look; yet, winking, there appears
Quick-shifting antics ugly in her eyes.   459
Such shadows are the weak brain's forgeries,   460
   Who, angry that the eyes fly from their lights,   461
   In darkness daunts them with more dreadful sights.

His hand, that yet remains upon her breast
(Rude ram, to batter such an ivory wall!)   464
May feel her heart (poor citizen) distressed,
Wounding itself to death, rise up and fall,
Beating her bulk, that his hand shakes withal.   467
   This moves in him more rage and lesser pity,
   To make the breach and enter this sweet city.

First like a trumpet doth his tongue begin
To sound a parley to his heartless foe;   471
Who o'er the white sheet peers her whiter chin,
The reason of this rash alarm to know,
Which he by dumb demeanor seeks to show;   474
   But she with vehement prayers urgeth still
   Under what color he commits this ill.   476

---

453 *taking* fright 459 *antics* grotesques 460 *shadows* shapes 461 *lights*
i.e. sight 464 *ram* battering-ram 467 *bulk* body 471 *heartless* timorous
474 *dumb demeanor* dumbshow 476 *color* pretext

Thus he replies : 'The color in thy face,
That even for anger makes the lily pale
And the red rose blush at her own disgrace,
Shall plead for me and tell my loving tale.
481   Under that color am I come to scale
      Thy never-conquerèd fort. The fault is thine,
      For those thine eyes betray thee unto mine.

'Thus I forestall thee, if thou mean to chide :
485   Thy beauty hath ensnared thee to this night,
486   Where thou with patience must my will abide,
My will that marks thee for my earth's delight,
Which I to conquer sought with all my might ;
      But as reproof and reason beat it dead,
      By thy bright beauty was it newly bred.

491   'I see what crosses my attempt will bring,
I know what thorns the growing rose defends,
I think the honey guarded with a sting ;
All this beforehand counsel comprehends,
But Will is deaf and hears no heedful friends :
      Only he hath an eye to gaze on Beauty,
      And dotes on what he looks, 'gainst law or duty.

'I have debated even in my soul
What wrong, what shame, what sorrow I shall breed ;
500   But nothing can affection's course control
Or stop the headlong fury of his speed.
502   I know repentant tears ensue the deed,
      Reproach, disdain, and deadly enmity ;
      Yet strive I to embrace mine infamy.'

---

481 *color* banner 485 *to this night* i.e. into this night's meeting 486 *will* sexual desire 491 *crosses* troubles 500 *affection's* passion's 502 *ensue* follow upon

This said, he shakes aloft his Roman blade,
Which, like a falcon tow'ring in the skies,
Coucheth the fowl below with his wings' shade,   507
Whose crooked beak threats if he mount he dies.
So under his insulting falchion lies
    Harmless Lucretia, marking what he tells
    With trembling fear, as fowl hear falcons' bells.

'Lucrece,' quoth he, 'this night I must enjoy thee.
If thou deny, then force must work my way;
For in thy bed I purpose to destroy thee.
That done, some worthless slave of thine I'll slay,
To kill thine honor with thy live's decay;   516
    And in thy dead arms do I mean to place him,
    Swearing I slew him, seeing thee embrace him.

'So thy surviving husband shall remain
The scornful mark of every open eye;
Thy kinsmen hang their heads at this disdain,   521
Thy issue blurred with nameless bastardy;
And thou, the author of their obloquy,
    Shalt have thy trespass cited up in rhymes
    And sung by children in succeeding times.

'But if thou yield, I rest thy secret friend;
The fault unknown is as a thought unacted.
A little harm done to a great good end
For lawful policy remains enacted.
The poisonous simple sometime is compacted   530
    In a pure compound; being so applied,
    His venom in effect is purified.

507 *Coucheth* makes cower 516 *live's* life's 521 *disdain* stain, disgrace
530 *simple* herb; *compacted* compounded

'Then, for thy husband and thy children's sake,
534 Tender my suit. Bequeath not to their lot
535 The shame that from them no device can take,
The blemish that will never be forgot;
537 Worse than a slavish wipe or birth-hour's blot;
    For marks descried in men's nativity
    Are nature's faults, not their own infamy.'

540 Here with a cockatrice' dead-killing eye
He rouseth up himself and makes a pause;
While she, the picture of pure piety,
543 Like a white hind under the gripe's sharp claws,
Pleads, in a wilderness where are no laws,
    To the rough beast that knows no gentle right
    Nor aught obeys but his foul appetite.

But when a black-faced cloud the world doth threat,
In his dim mist th' aspiring mountains hiding,
549 From earth's dark womb some gentle gust doth get,
Which blows these pitchy vapors from their biding,
551 Hind'ring their present fall by this dividing,
    So his unhallowed haste her words delays,
553   And moody Pluto winks while Orpheus plays.

Yet, foul night-waking cat, he doth but dally,
While in his hold-fast foot the weak mouse panteth.
556 Her sad behavior feeds his vulture folly,
557 A swallowing gulf that even in plenty wanteth.
His ear her prayers admits, but his heart granteth
559   No penetrable entrance to her plaining.
    Tears harden lust, though marble wear with raining.

---

534 *Tender* regard 535 *device* armorial figure 537 *wipe* brand-mark; *birth-hour's blot* birthmark 540 *cockatrice'* basilisk's (legendary serpent which killed with a look) 543 *gripe's* griffin's (?) 549 *doth get* is begot 551 *dividing* dispersal 553 *Pluto* ruler of the underworld, who was charmed by the lyre of Orpheus, husband of Eurydice; *winks* sleeps 556 *sad* grave; *vulture* ravenous 557 *gulf* belly 559 *plaining* complaining, lament

Her pity-pleading eyes are sadly fixèd
In the remorseless wrinkles of his face.   562
Her modest eloquence with sighs is mixèd,
Which to her oratory adds more grace.   564
She puts the period often from his place,   565
    And midst the sentence so her accent breaks
    That twice she doth begin ere once she speaks.

She conjures him by high almighty Jove,
By knighthood, gentry, and sweet friendship's oath,
By her untimely tears, her husband's love,
By holy human law and common troth,
By heaven and earth, and all the power of both,
    That to his borrowed bed he make retire
    And stoop to honor, not to foul desire.   574

Quoth she, 'Reward not hospitality
With such black payment as thou hast pretended;   576
Mud not the fountain that gave drink to thee;
Mar not the thing that cannot be amended.
End thy ill aim before thy shoot be ended.   579
    He is no woodman that doth bend his bow   580
    To strike a poor unseasonable doe.

'My husband is thy friend : for his sake spare me;
Thyself art mighty : for thine own sake leave me;
Myself a weakling : do not then ensnare me;
Thou look'st not like deceit : do not deceive me.
My sighs like whirlwinds labor hence to heave thee.   586
    If ever man were moved with woman's moans,
    Be movèd with my tears, my sighs, my groans;

---

562 *remorseless* pitiless   564 *oratory* pleading   565 *his place* i.e. its proper place (in broken utterance)   574 *stoop* bow, defer   576 *pretended* proposed
579 *shoot* act of shooting (perhaps with pun on homonymic 'suit')   580
woodman huntsman   586 *heave* move

'All which together, like a troubled ocean,
Beat at thy rocky and wrack-threat'ning heart,
To soften it with their continual motion;
592   For stones dissolved to water do convert.
O, if no harder than a stone thou art,
    Melt at my tears and be compassionate!
    Soft pity enters at an iron gate.

'In Tarquin's likeness I did entertain thee.
Hast thou put on his shape to do him shame?
To all the host of heaven I complain me.
Thou wrong'st his honor, wound'st his princely name.
Thou art not what thou seem'st; and if the same,
    Thou seem'st not what thou art, a god, a king;
    For kings like gods should govern everything.

603   'How will thy shame be seeded in thine age
When thus thy vices bud before thy spring?
If in thy hope thou dar'st do such outrage,
What dar'st thou not when once thou art a king?
O, be rememb'red, no outrageous thing
608   From vassal actors can be wiped away;
609   Then kings' misdeeds cannot be hid in clay.

'This deed will make thee only loved for fear;
But happy monarchs still are feared for love.
With foul offenders thou perforce must bear
When they in thee the like offenses prove.
614   If but for fear of this, thy will remove;
    For princes are the glass, the school, the book,
    Where subjects' eyes do learn, do read, do look.

---

592 *convert* change   **603** *be seeded* i.e. come to fruition   **608** *vassal actors* i.e. subjects who do it   **609** *in clay* i.e. even in death   **614** *thy will remove* dissuade your lust

'And wilt thou be the school where Lust shall learn?
Must he in thee read lectures of such shame?
Wilt thou be glass wherein it shall discern
Authority for sin, warrant for blame,
To privilege dishonor in thy name?
    Thou back'st reproach against long-living laud   **622**
    And mak'st fair reputation but a bawd.

'Hast thou command? By him that gave it thee,
From a pure heart command thy rebel will!
Draw not thy sword to guard iniquity,
For it was lent thee all that brood to kill.
Thy princely office how canst thou fulfill
    When, patterned by thy fault, foul Sin may say,
    He learned to sin, and thou didst teach the way?

'Think but how vile a spectacle it were
To view thy present trespass in another.
Men's faults do seldom to themselves appear;
Their own transgressions partially they smother.
This guilt would seem death-worthy in thy brother.
    O, how are they wrapped in with infamies
    That from their own misdeeds askaunce their eyes!   **637**

'To thee, to thee, my heaved-up hands appeal,
Not to seducing lust, thy rash relier.   **639**
I sue for exiled majesty's repeal;   **640**
Let him return, and flatt'ring thoughts retire.
His true respect will prison false desire   **642**
    And wipe the dim mist from thy doting eyne,
    That thou shalt see thy state, and pity mine.'

---

622 *back'st* support; *laud* praise   **637** *askaunce* avert   **639** *relier* thing relied
upon (?)   **640** *repeal* return from exile   **642** *respect* sense of decorum;
prison imprison

'Have done,' quoth he. 'My uncontrollèd tide
646 Turns not, but swells the higher by this let.
Small lights are soon blown out; huge fires abide
And with the wind in greater fury fret.
The petty streams that pay a daily debt
650   To their salt sovereign with their fresh falls' haste,
   Add to his flow, but alter not his taste.'

'Thou art,' quoth she, 'a sea, a sovereign king;
And, lo, there falls into thy boundless flood
Black lust, dishonor, shame, misgoverning,
Who seek to stain the ocean of thy blood.
If all these petty ills shall change thy good,
657   Thy sea within a puddle's womb is hearsèd,
   And not the puddle in thy sea dispersèd.

'So shall these slaves be king, and thou their slave;
Thou nobly base, they basely dignified;
Thou their fair life, and they thy fouler grave;
Thou loathèd in their shame, they in thy pride.
The lesser thing should not the greater hide.
   The cedar stoops not to the base shrub's foot,
   But low shrubs wither at the cedar's root.

'So let thy thoughts, low vassals to thy state.'
'No more,' quoth he. 'By heaven, I will not hear thee!
Yield to my love; if not, enforcèd hate,
Instead of love's coy touch, shall rudely tear thee.
670 That done, despitefully I mean to bear thee
   Unto the base bed of some rascal groom,
   To be thy partner in this shameful doom.'

---

646 *let* hindrance   650 *salt sovereign* i.e. the ocean; *falls'* flows'   657 *hearsèd* entombed

This said, he sets his foot upon the light,
For light and lust are deadly enemies;
Shame folded up in blind concealing night,
When most unseen, then most doth tyrannize.
The wolf hath seized his prey; the poor lamb cries,
    Till with her own white fleece her voice controlled   678
    Entombs her outcry in her lips' sweet fold;

For with the nightly linen that she wears
He pens her piteous clamors in her head,
Cooling his hot face in the chastest tears
That ever modest eyes with sorrow shed.
O, that prone lust should stain so pure a bed,
    The spots whereof, could weeping purify,
    Her tears should drop on them perpetually!

But she hath lost a dearer thing than life,
And he hath won what he would lose again.
This forcèd league doth force a further strife;
This momentary joy breeds months of pain;
This hot desire converts to cold disdain;
    Pure Chastity is rifled of her store,
    And Lust, the thief, far poorer than before.

Look, as the full-fed hound or gorgèd hawk,
Unapt for tender smell or speedy flight,   695
Make slow pursuit, or altogether balk   696
The prey wherein by nature they delight,
So surfeit-taking Tarquin fares this night:
    His taste delicious, in digestion souring,
    Devours his will, that lived by foul devouring.

678 *controlled* overpowered 695 *tender smell* weak scent 696 *balk* turn
from

701   O, deeper sin than bottomless conceit
         Can comprehend in still imagination !
703   Drunken Desire must vomit his receipt
         Ere he can see his own abomination.
705   While Lust is in his pride, no exclamation
            Can curb his heat or rein his rash desire
            Till, like a jade, Self-will himself doth tire.

         And then with lank and lean discolored cheek,
         With heavy eye, knit brow, and strengthless pace,
710   Feeble Desire, all recreant, poor, and meek,
711   Like to a bankrout beggar wails his case.
         The flesh being proud, Desire doth fight with Grace,
713   For there it revels ; and when that decays,
            The guilty rebel for remission prays.

         So fares it with this fault-full lord of Rome,
         Who this accomplishment so hotly chasèd ;
         For now against himself he sounds this doom,
         That through the length of times he stands disgracèd.
         Besides, his soul's fair temple is defacèd ;
            To whose weak ruins muster troops of cares,
721   To ask the spotted princess how she fares.

722   She says her subjects with foul insurrection
         Have battered down her consecrated wall,
724   And by their mortal fault brought in subjection
         Her immortality and made her thrall
         To living death and pain perpetual ;
727   Which in her prescience she controllèd still,
            But her foresight could not forestall their will.

---

701 *bottomless conceit* unlimited fancy   703 *his receipt* what he has received
705 *exclamation* protest   710 *recreant* beaten, cowed   711 *bankrout* bankrupt   713 *that* i.e. pride, lust   721 *spotted princess* i.e. besmirched soul
722 *subjects* i.e. senses (which should be subjects to the soul)   724 *mortal*
deadly; *in* into   727 *Which* who (i.e. the subject senses)

Ev'n in this thought through the dark night he stealeth,
A captive victor that hath lost in gain ;
Bearing away the wound that nothing healeth,
The scar that will despite of cure remain ;
Leaving his spoil perplexed in greater pain.
    She bears the load of lust he left behind,
    And he the burden of a guilty mind.

He like a thievish dog creeps sadly thence ;
She like a wearied lamb lies panting there.
He scowls, and hates himself for his offense ;
She desperate with her nails her flesh doth tear.
He faintly flies, sweating with guilty fear ;
    She stays, exclaiming on the direful night ;
    He runs, and chides his vanished loathed delight.

He thence departs a heavy convertite ;   743
She there remains a hopeless castaway.   744
He in his speed looks for the morning light ;
She prays she never may behold the day,
'For day,' quoth she, 'night's scapes doth open lay,   747
    And my true eyes have never practiced how
    To cloak offenses with a cunning brow.

'They think not but that every eye can see
The same disgrace which they themselves behold ;
And therefore would they still in darkness be,
To have their unseen sin remain untold ;
For they their guilt with weeping will unfold
    And grave, like water that doth eat in steel,   755
    Upon my cheeks what helpless shame I feel.'

---

743 *convertite* penitent   744 *castaway* lost soul   747 *scapes* misdeeds   755
grave engrave

Here she exclaims against repose and rest,
And bids her eyes hereafter still be blind.
She wakes her heart by beating on her breast,
And bids it leap from thence, where it may find
761 Some purer chest to close so pure a mind.
    Frantic with grief thus breathes she forth her spite
    Against the unseen secrecy of night:

'O comfort-killing Night, image of hell,
765 Dim register and notary of shame,
Black stage for tragedies and murders fell,
Vast sin-concealing chaos, nurse of blame,
Blind muffled bawd, dark harbor for defame!
    Grim cave of death, whisp'ring conspirator
770   With close-tongued treason and the ravisher!

'O hateful, vaporous, and foggy Night,
Since thou art guilty of my cureless crime,
Muster thy mists to meet the eastern light,
774 Make war against proportioned course of time;
Or if thou wilt permit the sun to climb
    His wonted height, yet ere he go to bed,
    Knit poisonous clouds about his golden head.

'With rotten damps ravish the morning air;
Let their exhaled unwholesome breaths make sick
780 The life of purity, the supreme fair,
781 Ere he arrive his weary noontide prick;
And let thy musty vapors march so thick
    That in their smoky ranks his smoth'red light
    May set at noon and make perpetual night.

761 *close* enclose   765 *notary* recorder   770 *close-tongued* secretive   774
proportioned orderly   780 *fair* i.e. the sun   781 *noontide prick* point of noon

'Were Tarquin Night, as he is but Night's child,
The silver-shining queen he would distain; 786
Her twinkling handmaids too, by him defiled,
Through Night's black bosom should not peep again.
So should I have co-partners in my pain;
    And fellowship in woe doth woe assuage,
    As palmers' chat makes short their pilgrimage; 791

'Where now I have no one to blush with me,
To cross their arms and hang their heads with mine,
To mask their brows and hide their infamy;
But I alone, alone must sit and pine,
Seasoning the earth with show'rs of silver brine,
    Mingling my talk with tears, my grief with groans,
    Poor wasting monuments of lasting moans.

'O Night, thou furnace of foul reeking smoke,
Let not the jealous Day behold that face 800
Which underneath thy black all-hiding cloak
Immodestly lies martyred with disgrace!
Keep still possession of thy gloomy place,
    That all the faults which in thy reign are made
    May likewise be sepulchered in thy shade!

'Make me not object to the telltale Day. 806
The light will show, charactered in my brow,
The story of sweet chastity's decay,
The impious breach of holy wedlock vow.
Yea, the illiterate, that know not how
    To cipher what is writ in learnèd books,
    Will quote my loathsome trespass in my looks. 812

786 *distain* stain 791 *palmers' chat* i.e. conversation among religious pilgrims 800 *jealous* i.e. censorious 806 *object* i.e. subject matter 812 *quote* note

'The nurse, to still her child, will tell my story
And fright her crying babe with Tarquin's name.
The orator, to deck his oratory,
Will couple my reproach to Tarquin's shame.
817 Feast-finding minstrels, tuning my defame,
    Will tie the hearers to attend each line,
    How Tarquin wrongèd me, I Collatine.

820 'Let my good name, that senseless reputation,
For Collatine's dear love be kept unspotted.
If that be made a theme for disputation,
The branches of another root are rotted,
And undeserved reproach to him allotted
    That is as clear from this attaint of mine
    As I ere this was pure to Collatine.

'O unseen shame, invisible disgrace!
828 O unfelt sore, crest-wounding private scar!
Reproach is stamped in Collatinus' face,
830 And Tarquin's eye may read the mot afar,
How he in peace is wounded, not in war.
    Alas, how many bear such shameful blows
    Which not themselves, but he that gives them knows!

'If, Collatine, thine honor lay in me,
From me by strong assault it is bereft;
My honey lost, and I, a drone-like bee,
Have no perfection of my summer left,
But robbed and ransacked by injurious theft.
    In thy weak hive a wand'ring wasp hath crept
    And sucked the honey which thy chaste bee kept.

---

817 *Feast-finding minstrels* i.e. minstrels who seek out festival occasions
820 *senseless* impalpable, spiritual (?) 828 *crest-wounding* i.e. that which
blots the escutcheon 830 *mot* motto

'Yet am I guilty of thy honor's wrack;
Yet for thy honor did I entertain him.
Coming from thee, I could not put him back,   843
For it had been dishonor to disdain him.
Besides, of weariness he did complain him
    And talked of virtue – O unlooked-for evil
    When virtue is profaned in such a devil!

'Why should the worm intrude the maiden bud?
Or hateful cuckoos hatch in sparrow's nests?
Or toads infect fair founts with venom mud?
Or tyrant folly lurk in gentle breasts?
Or kings be breakers of their own behests?   852
    But no perfection is so absolute
    That some impurity doth not pollute.

'The agèd man that coffers up his gold
Is plagued with cramps and gouts and painful fits,
And scarce hath eyes his treasure to behold,
But like still-pining Tantalus he sits
And useless barns the harvest of his wits,   859
    Having no other pleasure of his gain
    But torment that it cannot cure his pain.

'So then he hath it when he cannot use it,
And leaves it to be mast'red by his young,
Who in their pride do presently abuse it.
Their father was too weak, and they too strong,
To hold their cursèd-blessèd fortune long.
    The sweets we wish for turn to loathèd sours
    Even in the moment that we call them ours.

843 *put him back* repel him   852 *behests* commands, laws   859 *useless . . . wits* i.e. keeps uselessly in storage the product of his acumen

'Unruly blasts wait on the tender spring;
Unwholesome weeds take root with precious flow'rs;
The adder hisses where the sweet birds sing;
What Virtue breeds Iniquity devours.
We have no good that we can say is ours,
874   But ill-annexèd Opportunity
875   Or kills his life or else his quality.

'O Opportunity, thy guilt is great!
'Tis thou that execut'st the traitor's treason;
Thou sets the wolf where he the lamb may get;
Whoever plots the sin, thou point'st the season.
'Tis thou that spurn'st at right, at law, at reason;
    And in thy shady cell, where none may spy him,
    Sits Sin, to seize the souls that wander by him.

'Thou mak'st the vestal violate her oath;
Thou blow'st the fire when temperance is thawed;
Thou smother'st honesty, thou murd'rest troth.
Thou foul abettor, thou notorious bawd,
887   Thou plantest scandal and displacest laud.
    Thou ravisher, thou traitor, thou false thief,
    Thy honey turns to gall, thy joy to grief.

'Thy secret pleasure turns to open shame,
Thy private feasting to a public fast,
892   Thy smoothing titles to a ragged name,
Thy sug'red tongue to bitter wormwood taste:
Thy violent vanities can never last.
    How comes it then, vile Opportunity,
    Being so bad, such numbers seek for thee?

874 *ill-annexèd* evilly coupled 875 *Or* either; *his* its (i.e. good's) 887
displacest laud displant praise 892 *smoothing* flattering; *ragged* worn away,
disgraced

'When wilt thou be the humble suppliant's friend
And bring him where his suit may be obtainèd?
When wilt thou sort an hour great strifes to end?   899
Or free that soul which wretchedness hath chainèd?
Give physic to the sick, ease to the painèd?
 The poor, lame, blind, halt, creep, cry out for thee;
 But they ne'er meet with Opportunity.

'The patient dies while the physician sleeps;
The orphan pines while the oppressor feeds;
Justice is feasting while the widow weeps;
Advice is sporting while infection breeds.   907
Thou grant'st no time for charitable deeds:
 Wrath, envy, treason, rape, and murder's rages,
 Thy heinous hours wait on them as their pages.

'When Truth and Virtue have to do with thee,
A thousand crosses keep them from thy aid.   912
They buy thy help; but Sin ne'er gives a fee,
He gratis comes; and thou art well apaid
As well to hear as grant what he hath said.
 My Collatine would else have come to me
 When Tarquin did, but he was stayed by thee.

'Guilty thou art of murder and of theft,
Guilty of perjury and subornation,
Guilty of treason, forgery, and shift,   920
Guilty of incest, that abomination –
An accessary by thine inclination
 To all sins past and all that are to come,
 From the creation to the general doom.

---

899 *sort* appoint 907 *Advice is sporting* i.e. medical advice (or adviser) is engaged in amusement 912 *crosses* hindrances 920 *shift* fraud

925   'Misshapen Time, copesmate of ugly Night,
926   Swift subtle post, carrier of grisly care,
        Eater of youth, false slave to false delight,
928   Base watch of woes, sin's packhorse, virtue's snare!
        Thou nursest all, and murd'rest all that are.
          O, hear me then, injurious shifting Time;
          Be guilty of my death, since of my crime.

        'Why hath thy servant Opportunity
        Betrayed the hours thou gav'st me to repose?
        Cancelled my fortunes, and enchainèd me
        To endless date of never-ending woes?
936   Time's office is to fine the hate of foes,
          To eat up errors by opinion bred,
938   Not spend the dowry of a lawful bed.

        'Time's glory is to calm contending kings,
        To unmask falsehood and bring truth to light,
        To stamp the seal of time in agèd things,
942   To wake the morn and sentinel the night,
        To wrong the wronger till he render right,
944   To ruinate proud buildings with thy hours,
          And smear with dust their glitt'ring golden tow'rs;

        'To fill with wormholes stately monuments,
        To feed oblivion with decay of things,
        To blot old books and alter their contents,
949   To pluck the quills from ancient ravens' wings,
950   To dry the old oak's sap and cherish springs,
          To spoil antiquities of hammered steel
          And turn the giddy round of Fortune's wheel;

---

925 *copesmate* boon companion   926 *subtle post* sly messenger   928 *watch* crier   936 *fine* end   938 *spend* waste, dissipate   942 *sentinel* keep watch over, tell the hours of   944 *ruinate* i.e. reduce to ruins (and thus teach humility)   949 *pluck . . . wings* i.e. end the life even of the long-lived raven 950 *springs* saplings, new growth

'To show the beldame daughters of her daughter,
To make the child a man, the man a child,
To slay the tiger that doth live by slaughter,
To tame the unicorn and lion wild,
To mock the subtle in themselves beguiled,   957
    To cheer the ploughman with increaseful crops
    And waste huge stones with little water-drops.   959

'Why work'st thou mischief in thy pilgrimage,
Unless thou couldst return to make amends?
One poor retiring minute in an age   962
Would purchase thee a thousand thousand friends,
Lending him wit that to bad debtors lends.
    O this dread night, wouldst thou one hour come back,
    I could prevent this storm and shun thy wrack!

'Thou ceaseless lackey to Eternity,   967
With some mischance cross Tarquin in his flight.
Devise extremes beyond extremity   969
To make him curse this cursèd crimeful night.
Let ghastly shadows his lewd eyes affright,
    And the dire thought of his committed evil
    Shape every bush a hideous shapeless devil.

'Disturb his hours of rest with restless trances;   974
Afflict him in his bed with bedrid groans;
Let there bechance him pitiful mischances
To make him moan, but pity not his moans.
Stone him with hard'ned hearts harder than stones,
    And let mild women to him lose their mildness,
    Wilder to him than tigers in their wildness.

957 *subtle* crafty   959 *waste* wear away   962 *retiring minute* moment of
respite (allowing opportunity for a different choice)   967 *ceaseless lackey*
ever-present attendant   969 *extremes beyond extremity* i.e. inconceivably ex-
treme occasions   974 *trances* transports, fits

'Let him have time to tear his curlèd hair,
Let him have time against himself to rave,
Let him have time of Time's help to despair,
Let him have time to live a loathèd slave,
985   Let him have time a beggar's orts to crave,
    And time to see one that by alms doth live
    Disdain to him disdainèd scraps to give.

'Let him have time to see his friends his foes
And merry fools to mock at him resort;
Let him have time to mark how slow time goes
In time of sorrow, and how swift and short
His time of folly and his time of sport;
993   And ever let his unrecalling crime
    Have time to wail th' abusing of his time.

'O Time, thou tutor both to good and bad,
Teach me to curse him that thou taught'st this ill.
At his own shadow let the thief run mad,
Himself himself seek every hour to kill.
Such wretched hands such wretched blood should spill,
    For who so base would such an office have
1001   As sland'rous deathsman to so base a slave?

'The baser is he, coming from a king,
To shame his hope with deeds degenerate.
The mightier man, the mightier is the thing
That makes him honored or begets him hate;
For greatest scandal waits on greatest state.
    The moon being clouded presently is missed,
    But little stars may hide them when they list.

985 *orts* scraps   993 *unrecalling* irrevocable   1001 *sland'rous* disgraced

'The crow may bathe his coal-black wings in mire
And unperceived fly with the filth away;
But if the like the snow-white swan desire,
The stain upon his silver down will stay.
Poor grooms are sightless night, kings glorious day;   1013
    Gnats are unnoted wheresoe'er they fly,
    But eagles gazed upon with every eye.

'Out, idle words, servants to shallow fools,
Unprofitable sounds, weak arbitrators!   1017
Busy yourselves in skill-contending schools;   1018
Debate where leisure serves with full debaters;
To trembling clients be you mediators:
    For me, I force not argument a straw,   1021
    Since that my case is past the help of law.

'In vain I rail at Opportunity,
At Time, at Tarquin, and uncheerful Night;
In vain I cavil with mine infamy;
In vain I spurn at my confirmed despite: 1026
This helpless smoke of words doth me no right.
    The remedy indeed to do me good
    Is to let forth my foul defilèd blood.

'Poor hand, why quiver'st thou at this decree?
Honor thyself to rid me of this shame;
For if I die, my honor lives in thee;
But if I live, thou liv'st in my defame.
Since thou couldst not defend thy loyal dame
    And wast afeard to scratch her wicked foe,
    Kill both thyself and her for yielding so.'

1013 *sightless* unseen   1017 *arbitrators* i.e. compromisers   1018 *skill-contending schools* i.e. schoolmen's contests of skill   1021 *force . . . straw* i.e. place not the value of a straw upon argument   1026 *despite* wrong

This said, from her betumbled couch she starteth
To find some desp'rate instrument of death;
1039 But this no slaughterhouse no tool imparteth
To make more vent for passage of her breath;
Which, thronging through her lips, so vanisheth
    As smoke from Aetna that in air consumes
    Or that which from dischargèd cannon fumes.

'In vain,' quoth she, 'I live, and seek in vain
Some happy mean to end a hapless life.
1046 I feared by Tarquin's falchion to be slain,
Yet for the selfsame purpose seek a knife;
But when I feared I was a loyal wife.
    So am I now. – O no, that cannot be:
1050   Of that true type hath Tarquin rifled me.

'O, that is gone for which I sought to live,
And therefore now I need not fear to die.
To clear this spot by death, at least I give
1054 A badge of fame to slander's livery,
A dying life to living infamy.
    Poor helpless help, the treasure stol'n away,
    To burn the guiltless casket where it lay!

'Well, well, dear Collatine, thou shalt not know
The stainèd taste of violated troth.
I will not wrong thy true affection so,
To flatter thee with an infringèd oath.
1062 This bastard graff shall never come to growth:
    He shall not boast who did thy stock pollute
    That thou art doting father of his fruit.

1039 *imparteth* provides   **1046** *falchion* curved sword   **1050** *type* stamp
1054 *livery* garment, uniform (with *badge* of household worn on sleeve)
1062 *graff* graft

'Nor shall he smile at thee in secret thought,
Nor laugh with his companions at thy state;
But thou shalt know thy int'rest was not bought   1067
Basely with gold, but stol'n from forth thy gate.
For me, I am the mistress of my fate,
 And with my trespass never will dispense   1070
 Till life to death acquit my forced offense.   1071

'I will not poison thee with my attaint
Nor fold my fault in cleanly coined excuses;   1073
My sable ground of sin I will not paint
To hide the truth of this false night's abuses.
My tongue shall utter all; mine eyes, like sluices,
 As from a mountain spring that feeds a dale,
 Shall gush pure streams to purge my impure tale.'

By this, lamenting Philomele had ended
The well-tuned warble of her nightly sorrow,   1080
And solemn night with slow sad gait descended
To ugly hell; when, lo, the blushing morrow
Lends light to all fair eyes that light will borrow;
 But cloudy Lucrece shames herself to see
 And therefore still in night would cloist'red be.

Revealing day through every cranny spies
And seems to point her out where she sits weeping;
To whom she sobbing speaks: 'O eye of eyes
Why pry'st thou through my window? Leave thy peeping.
Mock with thy tickling beams eyes that are sleeping.
 Brand not my forehead with thy piercing light
 For day hath naught to do what's done by night.'

1067 *int'rest* claim, right 1070 *dispense* i.e. be reconciled 1071 *to death acquit* i.e. cancel by death 1073 *cleanly coined* brightly counterfeited

Thus cavils she with everything she sees.
1094 True grief is fond and testy as a child,
1095 Who wayward once, his mood with naught agrees.
1096 Old woes, not infant sorrows, bear them mild:
Continuance tames the one; the other wild,
Like an unpracticed swimmer plunging still,
With too much labor drowns for want of skill.

So she, deep drenchèd in a sea of care,
Holds disputation with each thing she views
And to herself all sorrow doth compare;
No object but her passion's strength renews;
1104 And as one shifts, another straight ensues.
Sometime her grief is dumb and hath no words;
Sometime 'tis mad and too much talk affords.

1107 The little birds that tune their morning's joy
Make her moans mad with their sweet melody:
1109 For mirth doth search the bottom of annoy;
Sad souls are slain in merry company;
Grief best is pleased with grief's society;
1112 True sorrow then is feelingly sufficed
1113 When with like semblance it is sympathized.

1114 'Tis double death to drown in ken of shore;
He ten times pines that pines beholding food;
To see the salve doth make the wound ache more;
Great grief grieves most at that would do it good;
Deep woes roll forward like a gentle flood,
Who, being stopped, the bounding banks o'erflows;
1120 Grief dallied with nor law nor limit knows.

1094 *fond* foolish; *testy* fretful   1095 *wayward once* i.e. once out of temper
1096 *them* themselves   1104 *shifts* yields place; *ensues* follows   1107 *tune*
sing   1109 *search* plumb; *annoy* sorrow   1112 *sufficed* satisfied   1113
sympathized matched   1114 *ken* sight   1120 *dallied with* teased

'You mocking birds,' quoth she, 'your tunes entomb
Within your hollow-swelling featherèd breasts,
And in my hearing be you mute and dumb;
My restless discord loves no stops nor rests: 1124
A woeful hostess brooks not merry guests.
    Relish your nimble notes to pleasing ears;   1126
    Distress likes dumps when time is kept with tears.   1127

'Come, Philomele, that sing'st of ravishment,   1128
Make thy sad grove in my dishevelled hair.
As the dank earth weeps at thy languishment,
So I at each sad strain will strain a tear
And with deep groans the diapason bear;   1132
    For burden-wise I'll hum on Tarquin still,
    While thou on Tereus descants better skill;   1134

'And whiles against a thorn thou bear'st thy part   1135
To keep thy sharp woes waking, wretched I,
To imitate thee well, against my heart
Will fix a sharp knife to affright mine eye;
Who, if it wink, shall thereon fall and die.   1139
    These means, as frets upon an instrument,
    Shall tune our heartstrings to true languishment.

'And for, poor bird, thou sing'st not in the day,
As shaming any eye should thee behold,
Some dark deep desert, seated from the way,   1144
That knows not parching heat nor freezing cold,
Will we find out; and there we will unfold
    To creatures stern sad tunes, to change their kinds.   1147
    Since men prove beasts, let beasts bear gentle minds.'

1124 *stops, rests* (1) musical pauses, (2) cessation   1126 *Relish* warble;
pleasing i.e. capable of being pleased   1127 *dumps* mournful airs   1128
Philomele (in classical myth, ravished by Tereus and transformed into the
nightingale)   1132 *diapason* bass accompaniment   1134 *descants better
skill* i.e. sings more skillfully (?), sings the intricate melody (?)   1135
bear'st sing'st   1139 *Who* which (i.e. her heart); *it wink* i.e. her eye close
1144 *seated from* situated out of   1147 *kinds* species

1149 As the poor frighted deer that stands at gaze,
Wildly determining which way to fly,
Or one encompassed with a winding maze
That cannot tread the way out readily,
So with herself is she in mutiny,
    To live or die which of the twain were better
1155   When life is shamed and death reproach's debtor.

'To kill myself,' quoth she, 'alack, what were it
But with my body my poor soul's pollution?
They that lose half with greater patience bear it
1159 Than they whose whole is swallowed in confusion.
1160 That mother tries a merciless conclusion
    Who, having two sweet babes, when death takes one,
    Will slay the other and be nurse to none.

'My body or my soul, which was the dearer
When the one, pure, the other made divine?
Whose love of either to myself was nearer
When both were kept for heaven and Collatine?
1167 Ay me! the bark pilled from the lofty pine,
    His leaves will wither and his sap decay:
    So must my soul, her bark being pilled away.

'Her house is sacked, her quiet interrupted,
Her mansion battered by the enemy;
Her sacred temple spotted, spoiled, corrupted,
1173 Grossly engirt with daring infamy.
Then let it not be called impiety
1175   If in this blemished fort I make some hole
    Through which I may convey this troubled soul.

1149 *at gaze* transfixed (hunting term) 1155 *death . . . debtor* i.e. suicide incurs reproach 1159 *confusion* destruction 1160 *conclusion* experiment 1167 *pilled* peeled 1173 *engirt* besieged; *daring* i.e. brazen 1175 *fort* i.e. body

'Yet die I will not till my Collatine
Have heard the cause of my untimely death;
That he may vow, in that sad hour of mine,
Revenge on him that made me stop my breath.
My stainèd blood to Tarquin I'll bequeath,
    Which, by him tainted, shall for him be spent
    And as his due writ in my testament.

'My honor I'll bequeath unto the knife
That wounds my body so dishonorèd.
'Tis honor to deprive dishonored life:
The one will live, the other being dead.
So of shame's ashes shall my fame be bred,
    For in my death I murder shameful scorn;
    My shame so dead, mine honor is new born.   *1190*

'Dear lord of that dear jewel I have lost,
What legacy shall I bequeath to thee?
My resolution, love, shall be thy boast,
By whose example thou revenged mayst be.
How Tarquin must be used, read it in me:
    Myself thy friend will kill myself thy foe,
    And for my sake serve thou false Tarquin so.

'This brief abridgment of my will I make:
My soul and body to the skies and ground;
My resolution, husband, do thou take;
Mine honor be the knife's that makes my wound;
My shame be his that did my fame confound;   *1202*
    And all my fame that lives disbursèd be
    To those that live and think no shame of me.

1202 *confound* destroy

1205 'Thou, Collatine, shalt oversee this will.
1206 (How was I overseen that thou shalt see it!)
1207 My blood shall wash the slander of mine ill;
 My live's foul deed, my life's fair end shall free it.
 Faint not, faint heart, but stoutly say, "So be it."
  Yield to my hand; my hand shall conquer thee:
  Thou dead, both die, and both shall victors be.'

 This plot of death when sadly she had laid
 And wiped the brinish pearl from her bright eyes,
1214 With untuned tongue she hoarsely calls her maid,
 Whose swift obedience to her mistress hies;
 For swift-winged duty with thought's feathers flies.
  Poor Lucrece' cheeks unto her maid seem so
  As winter meads when sun doth melt their snow.

1219 Her mistress she doth give demure good-morrow
 With soft-slow tongue, true mark of modesty,
1221 And sorts a sad look to her lady's sorrow,
1222 For why her face wore sorrow's livery;
 But durst not ask of her audaciously
  Why her two suns were cloud-eclipsèd so,
  Nor why her fair cheeks overwashed with woe.

 But as the earth doth weep, the sun being set,
 Each flower moist'ned like a melting eye,
 Even so the maid with swelling drops gan wet
1229 Her circled eyne, enforced by sympathy
 Of those fair suns set in her mistress' sky,
  Who in a salt-waved ocean quench their light,
  Which makes the maid weep like the dewy night.

1205 *oversee* execute, deal with 1206 *overseen* i.e. dealt with 1207 *wash*
wash away; *ill* sin 1214 *untuned* discordant 1219 *demure* meek 1221
sorts matches 1222 *For why* because 1229 *circled* dark-circled (?),
rounded (?); *eyne* eyes

A pretty while these pretty creatures stand,
Like ivory conduits coral cisterns filling.   1234
One justly weeps, the other takes in hand   1235
No cause, but company, of her drops spilling.
Their gentle sex to weep are often willing,
    Grieving themselves to guess at others' smarts,   1238
    And then they drown their eyes or break their hearts.

For men have marble, women waxen minds,   1240
And therefore are they formed as marble will.   1241
The weak oppressed, th' impression of strange kinds
Is formed in them by force, by fraud, or skill.
Then call them not the authors of their ill,
    No more than wax shall be accounted evil
    Wherein is stamped the semblance of a devil.

Their smoothness, like a goodly champain plain,   1247
Lays open all the little worms that creep;   1248
In men, as in a rough-grown grove, remain
Cave-keeping evils that obscurely sleep.   1250
Through crystal walls each little mote will peep.   1251
    Though men can cover crimes with bold stern looks,
    Poor women's faces are their own faults' books.

No man inveigh against the witherèd flow'r,
But chide rough winter that the flow'r hath killed.
Not that devoured, but that which doth devour,
Is worthy blame. O, let it not be hild   1257
Poor women's faults that they are so fulfilled   1258
    With men's abuses : those proud lords to blame   1259
    Make weak-made women tenants to their shame.

1234 *coral cisterns* i.e. their reddened eyes (?) 1235 *takes in hand* acknow-
ledges 1238 *to guess at* i.e. in mere conjecture of 1240 *waxen* i.e. yielding
to impressions 1241 *will* i.e. will have them formed 1247 *champain*
level and fertile 1248 *Lays open* reveals; *worms* reptiles 1250 *Cave-
keeping* inhabiting caves 1251 *mote* speck 1257 *hild* held 1258 *fulfilled* filled 1259 *abuses* misdemeanors

1261   The precedent whereof in Lucrece view,
1262   Assailed by night with circumstances strong
       Of present death, and shame that might ensue
       By that her death, to do her husband wrong.
       Such danger to resistance did belong
1266   That dying fear through all her body spread;
1267   And who cannot abuse a body dead?

1268   By this, mild patience bid fair Lucrece speak
1269   To the poor counterfeit of her complaining.
       'My girl,' quoth she, 'on what occasion break
       Those tears from thee that down thy cheeks are raining?
1272   If thou dost weep for grief of my sustaining,
       Know, gentle wench, it small avails my mood.
       If tears could help, mine own would do me good.

       'But tell me, girl, when went' (and there she stayed
       Till after a deep groan) 'Tarquin from hence?'
       'Madam, ere I was up,' replied the maid,
       'The more to blame my sluggard negligence.
       Yet with the fault I thus far can dispense –
       Myself was stirring ere the break of day,
       And ere I rose was Tarquin gone away.

       'But, lady, if your maid may be so bold,
1283   She would request to know your heaviness.'
       'O, peace,' quoth Lucrece. 'If it should be told,
       The repetition cannot make it less;
       For more it is than I can well express,
       And that deep torture may be called a hell
       When more is felt than one hath power to tell.

1261 *precedent* example 1262 *with . . . strong* i.e. under threat 1266 *dying* i.e. paralyzing 1267 *abuse* misuse 1268 *this* i.e. this time 1269 *counterfeit* copy, mirror 1272 *of my sustaining* i.e. which I sustain 1283 *know* i.e. learn the reason for

'Go get me hither paper, ink, and pen.
Yet save that labor, for I have them here.
What should I say? One of my husband's men
Bid thou be ready, by and by, to bear
A letter to my lord, my love, my dear.
　　Bid him with speed prepare to carry it;
　　The cause craves haste, and it will soon be writ.'

Her maid is gone, and she prepares to write,
First hovering o'er the paper with her quill.
Conceit and grief an eager combat fight; 1298
What wit sets down is blotted straight with will. 1299
This is too curious good, this blunt and ill. 1300
　　Much like a press of people at a door,
　　Throng her inventions, which shall go before.

At last she thus begins: 'Thou worthy lord
Of that unworthy wife that greeteth thee,
Health to thy person. Next vouchsafe t' afford
(If ever, love, thy Lucrece thou wilt see)
Some present speed to come and visit me.
　　So I commend me, from our house in grief.
　　My woes are tedious, though my words are brief.' 1309

Here folds she up the tenure of her woe, 1310
Her certain sorrow writ uncertainly.
By this short schedule Collatine may know 1312
Her grief, but not her grief's true quality.
She dares not thereof make discovery,
　　Lest he should hold it her own gross abuse 1315
　　Ere she with blood had stained her stained excuse. 1316

1298 *Conceit* i.e. the conception of what she will write　1299 *wit* i.e. the
intellectual faculty; *blotted* cancelled　1300 *curious* ingeniously　1309
tedious prolonged　1310 *tenure* brief statement　1312 *schedule* summary
1315 *gross abuse* i.e. willful wrongdoing　1316 *stained excuse* i.e. explana-
tion of her stain

Besides, the life and feeling of her passion
She hoards, to spend when he is by to hear her,
When sighs and groans and tears may grace the fashion
Of her disgrace, the better so to clear her
From that suspicion which the world might bear her.
1322   To shun this blot, she would not blot the letter
     With words till action might become them better.

To see sad sights moves more than hear them told,
For then the eye interprets to the ear
1326 The heavy motion that it doth behold
When every part a part of woe doth bear.
'Tis but a part of sorrow that we hear.
1329   Deep sounds make lesser noise than shallow fords,
     And sorrow ebbs, being blown with wind of words.

Her letter now is sealed, and on it writ,
'At Ardea to my lord with more than haste.'
The post attends, and she delivers it,
Charging the sour-faced groom to hie as fast
1335 As lagging fowls before the Northern blast.
     Speed more than speed but dull and slow she deems:
     Extremity still urgeth such extremes.

1338 The homely villain cursies to her low;
1339 And, blushing on her, with a steadfast eye,
Receives the scroll without or yea or no
And forth with bashful innocence doth hie.
But they whose guilt within their bosoms lie
     Imagine every eye beholds their blame;
     For Lucrece thought he blushed to see her shame,

1322 *blot . . . blot* disgrace . . . mar   1326 *heavy motion* sad action   1329 *sounds* soundings, levels of water   1335 *lagging* i.e. those tardy in their migratory flight   1338 *villain* serf; *cursies* genuflects   1339 *on her* i.e. in awe of her

When, seely groom, God wot it was defect 1345
Of spirit, life, and bold audacity. 1346
Such harmless creatures have a true respect 1347
To talk in deeds, while others saucily
Promise more speed, but do it leisurely.
 Even so this pattern of the worn-out age 1350
 Pawned honest looks, but laid no words to gage. 1351

His kindled duty kindled her mistrust,
That two red fires in both their faces blazèd.
She thought he blushed as knowing Tarquin's lust,
And, blushing with him, wistly on him gazèd; 1355
Her earnest eye did make him more amazèd.
 The more she saw the blood his cheeks replenish,
 The more she thought he spied in her some blemish.

But long she thinks till he return again, 1359
And yet the duteous vassal scarce is gone.
The weary time she cannot entertain, 1361
For now 'tis stale to sigh, to weep and groan.
So woe hath wearied woe, moan tirèd moan,
 That she her plaints a little while doth stay, 1364
 Pausing for means to mourn some newer way.

At last she calls to mind where hangs a piece
Of skillful painting, made for Priam's Troy, 1367
Before the which is drawn the power of Greece, 1368
For Helen's rape the city to destroy,
Threat'ning cloud-kissing Ilion with annoy; 1370
 Which the conceited painter drew so proud 1371
 As heaven, it seemed, to kiss the turrets bowed.

1345 *seely* simple   1346 *life* liveliness   1347 *respect* care   1350 *worn-out age* i.e. the good old days (of faithful service)   1351 *Pawned* offered as security; *gage* guaranty   1355 *wistly* meaningfully   1359 *long* i.e. it is a long time   1361 *entertain* occupy   1364 *stay* restrain   1367 *made for* depicting   1368 *power* army   1370 *cloud-kissing Ilion* i.e. high-towered Troy; *annoy* injury   1371 *conceited* inventive

A thousand lamentable objects there,
1374 In scorn of nature, art gave liveless life.
Many a dry drop seemed a weeping tear
Shed for the slaught'red husband by the wife.
1377 The red blood reeked, to show the painter's strife;
And dying eyes gleamed forth their ashy lights,
Like dying coals burnt out in tedious nights.

1380 There might you see the laboring pioner
Begrimed with sweat, and smearèd all with dust;
And from the tow'rs of Troy there would appear
The very eyes of men through loopholes thrust,
1384 Gazing upon the Greeks with little lust.
1385 Such sweet observance in this work was had
That one might see those far-off eyes look sad.

In great commanders grace and majesty
You might behold triumphing in their faces;
1389 In youth, quick bearing and dexterity;
And here and there the painter interlaces
Pale cowards marching on with trembling paces,
1392 Which heartless peasants did so well resemble
That one would swear he saw them quake and tremble.

In Ajax and Ulysses, O, what art
Of physiognomy might one behold!
1396 The face of either ciphered either's heart;
Their face their manners most expressly told:
In Ajax' eyes blunt rage and rigor rolled;
But the mild glance that sly Ulysses lent
1400 Showed deep regard and smiling government.

1374 *In scorn of* i.e. in defiant rivalry with; *liveless* inanimate   1377 *strife* effort   1380 *pioner* engineer, sapper   1384 *lust* liking   1385 *sweet observance* i.e. loving attention to detail   1389 *quick bearing* lively deportment   1392 *heartless* uncourageous   1396 *ciphered* expressed   1400 *deep regard* i.e. profundity; *smiling government* i.e. diplomatic skill

There pleading might you see grave Nestor stand,
As 'twere encouraging the Greeks to fight,
Making such sober action with his hand   1403
That it beguiled attention, charmed the sight.
In speech it seemed his beard, all silver white,
 Wagged up and down, and from his lips did fly   1406
 Thin winding breath, which purled up to the sky.   1407

About him were a press of gaping faces
Which seemed to swallow up his sound advice,
All jointly list'ning, but with several graces,
As if some mermaid did their ears entice,   1411
Some high, some low – the painter was so nice.   1412
 The scalps of many, almost hid behind,
 To jump up higher seemed, to mock the mind.   1414

Here one man's hand leaned on another's head,
His nose being shadowed by his neighbor's ear;
Here one, being thronged, bears back, all boll'n and red; 1417
Another, smothered, seems to pelt and swear;   1418
And in their rage such signs of rage they bear
 As, but for loss of Nestor's golden words,
 It seemed they would debate with angry swords.

For much imaginary work was there;
Conceit deceitful, so compact, so kind,   1423
That for Achilles' image stood his spear,
Griped in an armèd hand; himself behind
Was left unseen, save to the eye of mind:
 A hand, a foot, a face, a leg, a head
 Stood for the whole to be imaginèd.

1403 *action* gesture   1406 *Wagged* waved (non-humorous)   1407 *purled*
curled   1411 *mermaid* i.e. siren   1412 *Some . . . low* some tall and some
short; *nice* precise   1414 *mock* vainly tempt (so the spectator of the picture
might see those hidden in the rear)   1417 *thronged* crowded; *boll'n* swollen
1418 *pelt* scold   1423 *Conceit* contrivance; *compact* economical; *kind*
natural

And from the walls of strong-besiegèd Troy
When their brave hope, bold Hector, marchèd to field,
Stood many Troyan mothers, sharing joy
To see their youthful sons bright weapons wield;
1433   And to their hope they such odd action yield
    That through their light joy seemèd to appear
    (Like bright things stained) a kind of heavy fear.

1436   And from the strond of Dardan, where they fought,
1437   To Simois' reedy banks the red blood ran,
Whose waves to imitate the battle sought
With swelling ridges; and their ranks began
1440   To break upon the gallèd shore, and than
    Retire again, till, meeting greater ranks,
    They join, and shoot their foam at Simois' banks.

To this well-painted piece is Lucrece come,
1444   To find a face where all distress is stelled.
Many she sees where cares have carvèd some,
But none where all distress and dolor dwelled
Till she despairing Hecuba beheld,
    Staring on Priam's wounds with her old eyes,
    Which bleeding under Pyrrhus' proud foot lies.

1450   In her the painter had anatomized
Time's ruin, beauty's wrack, and grim care's reign;
1452   Her cheeks with chops and wrinkles were disguised;
Of what she was no semblance did remain.
Her blue blood, changed to black in every vein,
    Wanting the spring that those shrunk pipes had fed,
    Showed life imprisoned in a body dead.

1433 *odd action* contrary gestures; *yield* lend   1436 *strond of Dardan*
shore of Troas   1437 *Simois* river flowing from Mt Ida   1440 *gallèd*
eroded; *than* then   1444 *stelled* engraved   1450 *anatomized* laid open
1452 *chops* chapping; *disguised* disfigured

On this sad shadow Lucrece spends her eyes
And shapes her sorrow to the beldame's woes,　　　1458
Who nothing wants to answer her but cries
And bitter words to ban her cruel foes.　　　1460
The painter was no god to lend her those ;
　　And therefore Lucrece swears he did her wrong
　　To give her so much grief and not a tongue.

'Poor instrument,' quoth she, 'without a sound :
I'll tune thy woes with my lamenting tongue,　　　1465
And drop sweet balm in Priam's painted wound,
And rail on Pyrrhus that hath done him wrong,
And with my tears quench Troy that burns so long,
　　And with my knife scratch out the angry eyes
　　Of all the Greeks that are thine enemies.

'Show me the strumpet that began this stir,　　　1471
That with my nails her beauty I may tear.
Thy heat of lust, fond Paris, did incur　　　1473
This load of wrath that burning Troy doth bear.
Thy eye kindled the fire that burneth here,
　　And here in Troy, for trespass of thine eye,
　　The sire, the son, the dame and daughter die.

'Why should the private pleasure of some one
Become the public plague of many moe ?　　　1479
Let sin, alone committed, light alone
Upon his head that hath transgressèd so ;
Let guiltless souls be freed from guilty woe.
　　For one's offense why should so many fall,
　　To plague a private sin in general ?　　　1484

1458 *beldame's* aged woman's　1460 *ban* curse　1465 *tune* voice　1471
stir war　1473 *fond* foolish　1479 *moe* more　1484 *plague* i.e. punish; *in
general* i.e. on the general public

'Lo, here weeps Hecuba, here Priam dies,
1486 Here manly Hector faints, here Troilus sounds,
Here friend by friend in bloody channel lies,
1488 And friend to friend gives unadvisèd wounds,
And one man's lust these many lives confounds.
  Had doting Priam checked his son's desire,
  Troy had been bright with fame, and not with fire.'

Here feelingly she weeps Troy's painted woes,
For sorrow, like a heavy hanging bell,
Once set on ringing, with his own weight goes;
Then little strength rings out the doleful knell.
So Lucrece, set awork, sad tales doth tell
1497   To pencilled pensiveness and colored sorrow:
  She lends them words, and she their looks doth borrow.

1499 She throws her eyes about the painting round,
And who she finds forlorn she doth lament.
1501 At last she sees a wretched image bound
1502 That piteous looks to Phrygian shepherds lent.
His face, though full of cares, yet showed content;
1504   Onward to Troy with the blunt swains he goes,
1505   So mild that patience seemed to scorn his woes.

In him the painter labored with his skill
1507 To hide deceit, and give the harmless show
An humble gait, calm looks, eyes wailing still,
1509 A brow unbent that seemed to welcome woe,
Cheeks neither red nor pale, but mingled so
  That blushing red no guilty instance gave
  Nor ashy pale the fear that false hearts have;

1486 *sounds* swoons 1488 *unadvisèd* unintentional 1497 *pencilled, colored*
painted 1499 *round* all around 1501 *wretched image* i.e. of the traitor
Sinon 1502 *piteous . . . lent* i.e. drew looks of pity from Phrygian shepherds
1504 *blunt* rude 1505 *patience . . . scorn* i.e. his patience seemed to make
light of 1507 *show* appearance (affected by Sinon) 1509 *unbent* unfrown-
ing

But, like a constant and confirmèd devil,
He entertained a show so seeming just,   1514
And therein so ensconced his secret evil,
That jealousy itself could not mistrust   1516
False creeping craft and perjury should thrust
    Into so bright a day such black-faced storms
    Or blot with hell-born sin such saintlike forms.

The well-skilled workman this mild image drew
For perjured Sinon, whose enchanting story   1521
The credulous old Priam after slew;
Whose words like wildfire burnt the shining glory
Of rich-built Ilion, that the skies were sorry,
    And little stars shot from their fixèd places
    When their glass fell wherein they viewed their faces. 1526

This picture she advisedly perused   1527
And chid the painter for his wondrous skill,
Saying, some shape in Sinon's was abused;   1529
So fair a form lodged not a mind so ill.
And still on him she gazed, and gazing still,
    Such signs of truth in his plain face she spied
    That she concludes the picture was belied.   1533

'It cannot be,' quoth she, 'that so much guile' –
She would have said 'can lurk in such a look';
But Tarquin's shape came in her mind the while
And from her tongue 'can lurk' from 'cannot' took.
'It cannot be' she in that sense forsook   1538
    And turned it thus: 'It cannot be, I find,
    But such a face should bear a wicked mind;

1514 *entertained a show* i.e. adopted an appearance   1516 *jealousy* suspicion
1521 *enchanting story* i.e. seductive lie   1526 *glass* mirror (i.e. glittering
Troy)   1527 *advisedly* thoughtfully   1529 *some shape* i.e. the figure of
someone else; *abused* traduced   1533 *belied* proved false   1538 *that sense*
i.e. the sense originally intended

'For even as subtile Sinon here is painted,
So sober-sad, so weary, and so mild
(As if with grief or travail he had fainted),
1544   To me came Tarquin armèd, to beguiled
With outward honesty, but yet defiled
    With inward vice. As Priam him did cherish,
    So did I Tarquin; so my Troy did perish.

'Look, look how list'ning Priam wets his eyes
1549   To see those borrowed tears that Sinon sheeds!
Priam, why art thou old, and yet not wise?
For every tear he falls a Troyan bleeds.
His eye drops fire, no water thence proceeds.
    Those round clear pearls of his that move thy pity
    Are balls of quenchless fire to burn thy city.

'Such devils steal effects from lightless hell,
For Sinon in his fire doth quake with cold
And in that cold hot burning fire doth dwell.
1558   These contraries such unity do hold
1559   Only to flatter fools and make them bold.
    So Priam's trust false Sinon's tears doth flatter
    That he finds means to burn his Troy with water.'

Here, all enraged, such passion her assails
That patience is quite beaten from her breast.
She tears the senseless Sinon with her nails,
1565   Comparing him to that unhappy guest
Whose deed hath made herself herself detest.
    At last she smilingly with this gives o'er:
    'Fool, fool!' quoth she, 'his wounds will not be sore.'

1544 *armèd* equipped; *beguiled* beguile (with the superfluous 'd' providing a rhyme)   1549 *borrowed* i.e. false, not truly his; *sheeds* sheds   1558 *hold* maintain   1559 *flatter . . . bold* i.e. deceive fools and give them confidence   1565 *unhappy* unlucky, fatal

Thus ebbs and flows the current of her sorrow,
And time doth weary time with her complaining.
She looks for night, and then she longs for morrow,
And both she thinks too long with her remaining.
Short time seems long in sorrow's sharp sustaining; 1573
   Though woe be heavy, yet it seldom sleeps, 1574
   And they that watch see time how slow it creeps;

Which all this time hath overslipped her thought 1576
That she with painted images hath spent,
Being from the feeling of her own grief brought
By deep surmise of others' detriment, 1579
Losing her woes in shows of discontent. 1580
   It easeth some, though none it ever curèd,
   To think their dolor others have endurèd.

But now the mindful messenger, come back,
Brings home his lord and other company;
Who finds his Lucrece clad in mourning black,
And round about her tear-distainèd eye 1586
Blue circles streamed, like rainbows in the sky.
   These water-galls in her dim element 1588
   Foretell new storms to those already spent.

Which when her sad-beholding husband saw,
Amazedly in her sad face he stares.
Her eyes, though sod in tears, looked red and raw, 1592
Her lively color killed with deadly cares.
He hath no power to ask her how she fares;
   Both stood, like old acquaintance in a trance,
   Met far from home, wond'ring each other's chance. 1596

1573 *in . . . sustaining* in the sharp sorrow sustained   1574 *heavy* (1) burdensome, (2) sleepy   1576 *overslipped her thought* passed unnoticed   1579 *surmise* contemplation   1580 *shows* representations (i.e. of the woes of Troy)   1586 *tear-distainèd* tear-stained   1588 *water-galls* fragmentary rainbows (presaging stormy weather); *element* sky   1592 *sod* sodden 1596 *wond'ring . . . chance* i.e. wondering at each other's fortune

At last he takes her by the bloodless hand
1598 And thus begins : 'What uncouth ill event
Hath thee befall'n, that thou dost trembling stand ?
1600 Sweet love, what spite hath thy fair color spent ?
Why art thou thus attired in discontent ?
1602   Unmask, dear dear, this moody heaviness
        And tell thy grief, that we may give redress.'

1604 Three times with sighs she gives her sorrow fire
Ere once she can discharge one word of woe.
At length addressed to answer his desire,
She modestly prepares to let them know
Her honor is ta'en prisoner by the foe,
1609   While Collatine and his consorted lords
        With sad attention long to hear her words.

And now this pale swan in her wat'ry nest
1612 Begins the sad dirge of her certain ending :
'Few words,' quoth she, 'shall fit the trespass best
Where no excuse can give the fault amending.
1615 In me moe woes than words are now depending,
        And my laments would be drawn out too long
        To tell them all with one poor tirèd tongue.

'Then be this all the task it hath to say :
1619 Dear husband, in the interest of thy bed
A stranger came and on that pillow lay
Where thou wast wont to rest thy weary head ;
And what wrong else may be imaginèd
        By foul enforcement might be done to me,
        From that, alas, thy Lucrece is not free.

1598 *uncouth* strange   1600 *spent* dispersed   1602 *Unmask* disclose   1604
fire i.e. the ignition needed to discharge ancient firearms   1609 *consorted*
associated   1612 *certain ending* impending death   1615 *moe* more;
depending impending   1619 *interest* possession

'For in the dreadful dead of dark midnight
With shining falchion in my chamber came
A creeping creature with a flaming light
And softly cried, "Awake, thou Roman dame,
And entertain my love; else lasting shame
   On thee and thine this night I will inflict,
   If thou my love's desire do contradict.   1631

'"For some hard-favored groom of thine," quoth he,
"Unless thou yoke thy liking to my will,
I'll murder straight, and then I'll slaughter thee
And swear I found you where you did fulfill
The loathsome act of lust, and so did kill
   The lechers in their deed. This act will be
   My fame and thy perpetual infamy."

'With this I did begin to start and cry;
And then against my heart he set his sword,
Swearing, unless I took all patiently,
I should not live to speak another word.
So should my shame still rest upon record,
   And never be forgot in mighty Rome
   Th' adulterate death of Lucrece and her groom.

'Mine enemy was strong, my poor self weak
And far the weaker with so strong a fear.
My bloody judge forbod my tongue to speak;   1648
No rightful plea might plead for justice there.
His scarlet lust came evidence to swear
   That my poor beauty had purloined his eyes;
   And when the judge is robbed, the prisoner dies.

1631 *contradict* i.e. deny, counter   1648 *forbod* forbade

'O, teach me how to make mine own excuse,
Or at the least this refuge let me find :
Though my gross blood be stained with this abuse,
Immaculate and spotless is my mind ;
That was not forced ; that never was inclined
    To accessary yieldings, but still pure
    Doth in her poisoned closet yet endure.'

1660 Lo, here, the hopeless merchant of this loss,
With head declined and voice dammed up with woe,
With sad-set eyes and wreathèd arms across,
From lips new waxen pale begins to blow
The grief away that stops his answer so.
    But, wretched as he is, he strives in vain ;
    What he breathes out his breath drinks up again.

1667 As through an arch the violent roaring tide
Outruns the eye that doth behold his haste,
Yet in the eddy boundeth in his pride
Back to the strait that forced him on so fast ;
In rage sent out, recalled in rage being past :
1672   Even so his sighs, his sorrows, make a saw,
    To push grief on, and back the same grief draw.

Which speechless woe of his poor she attendeth
1675 And his untimely frenzy thus awaketh :
'Dear lord, thy sorrow to my sorrow lendeth
Another power, no flood by raining slaketh ;
1678 My woe too sensible thy passion maketh
    More feeling-painful. Let it then suffice
    To drown one woe, one pair of weeping eyes.

1660 *merchant . . . loss* i.e. Collatine, seen as a merchant whose ship has been wrecked 1667 *arch* (such as those of London Bridge, which provide the following image of current and back-current swirls) 1672 *saw* i.e. back-and-forth or sawlike motion 1675 *his . . . awaketh* i.e. breaks into his untimely trance 1678 *too sensible* i.e. already too sensitive

'And for my sake when I might charm thee so,   1681
For she that was thy Lucrece (now attend me)
Be suddenly revengèd on my foe,
Thine, mine, his own : suppose thou dost defend me
From what is past – the help that thou shalt lend me
   Comes all too late, yet let the traitor die ;
   For sparing justice feeds iniquity.

'But ere I name him, you fair lords,' quoth she,
Speaking to those that came with Collatine,
'Shall plight your honorable faiths to me
With swift pursuit to venge this wrong of mine ;
For 'tis a meritorious fair design
   To chase injustice with revengeful arms.
   Knights by their oaths should right poor ladies' harms.'

At this request, with noble disposition
Each present lord began to promise aid,
As bound in knighthood to her imposition,
Longing to hear the hateful foe bewrayed.   1698
But she, that yet her sad task hath not said,   1699
   The protestation stops. 'O, speak !' quoth she,
   'How may this forcèd stain be wiped from me ?   1701

'What is the quality of my offense,   1702
Being constrained with dreadful circumstance ?
May my pure mind with the foul act dispense,   1704
My low-declinèd honor to advance ?   1705
May any terms acquit me from this chance ?
   The poisonèd fountain clears itself again ;
   And why not I from this compellèd stain ?'

1681 *so* as such (i.e. as her former self implied in *my sake*)   1698 *bewrayed*
discovered   1699 *yet . . . said* i.e. had not yet finished this sad task of saying
1701 *forcèd* imposed by force   1702 *quality* nature   1704 *dispense* be
reconciled   1705 *advance* raise

With this they all at once began to say,
Her body's stain her mind untainted clears;
While with a joyless smile she turns away
The face, that map which deep impression bears
Of hard misfortune, carved in it with tears.
    'No, no!' quoth she, 'no dame hereafter living
    By my excuse shall claim excuse's giving.'

Here with a sigh as if her heart would break
She throws forth Tarquin's name: 'He, he!' she says,
But more than 'he' her poor tongue could not speak,
1719   Till after many accents and delays,
1720   Untimely breathings, sick and short assays,
        She utters this: 'He, he! fair lords, 'tis he
        That guides this hand to give this wound to me.'

Even here she sheathèd in her harmless breast
A harmful knife, that thence her soul unsheathèd.
1725   That blow did bail it from the deep unrest
Of that polluted prison where it breathèd.
Her contrite sighs unto the clouds bequeathèd
1728   Her wingèd sprite, and through her wounds doth fly
1729   Live's lasting date from cancelled destiny.

Stone-still, astonished with this deadly deed,
Stood Collatine and all his lordly crew,
Till Lucrece' father, that beholds her bleed,
Himself on her self-slaught'red body threw,
And from the purple fountain Brutus drew
        The murd'rous knife, and, as it left the place,
        Her blood, in poor revenge, held it in chase;

1719 *accents* utterances   1720 *assays* attempts   1725 *bail* release   1728 *sprite* spirit   1729 *Live's . . . date* i.e. eternal life; *cancelled destiny* i.e. the termination of earthly life

And bubbling from her breast, it doth divide
In two slow rivers, that the crimson blood
Circles her body in on every side,
Who, like a late-sacked island, vastly stood   1740
Bare and unpeopled in this fearful flood.
    Some of her blood still pure and red remained,
    And some looked black, and that false Tarquin stained.

About the mourning and congealèd face
Of that black blood a wat'ry rigoll goes,   1745
Which seems to weep upon the tainted place;
And ever since, as pitying Lucrece' woes,
Corrupted blood some watery token shows,
    And blood untainted still doth red abide,
    Blushing at that which is so putrefied.

'Daughter, dear daughter!' old Lucretius cries,
'That life was mine which thou hast here deprivèd.
If in the child the father's image lies,
Where shall I live now Lucrece is unlivèd?
Thou wast not to this end from me derivèd.
    If children predecease progenitors,
    We are their offspring, and they none of ours.

'Poor broken glass, I often did behold   1758
In thy sweet semblance my old age new born;
But now that fresh fair mirror, dim and old,
Shows me a bare-boned death by time outworn.   1761
O, from thy cheeks my image thou hast torn
    And shivered all the beauty of my glass,
    That I no more can see what once I was.

1740 *late-sacked* recently pillaged; *vastly stood* i.e. rose high above   **1745**
wat'ry rigoll i.e. the rim of serum which separates from coagulated blood
1758 *glass* mirror   **1761** *death* i.e. death's-head, skull

'O time, cease thou thy course, and last no longer,
If they surcease to be that should survive.
Shall rotten death make conquest of the stronger
And leave the falt'ring feeble souls alive?
The old bees die, the young possess their hive.
    Then live, sweet Lucrece, live again and see
    Thy father die, and not thy father thee.'

By this, starts Collatine as from a dream
And bids Lucretius give his sorrow place;
1774   And then in key-cold Lucrece' bleeding stream
1775   He falls, and bathes the pale fear in his face,
And counterfeits to die with her a space;
    Till manly shame bids him possess his breath
    And live to be revengèd on her death.

The deep vexation of his inward soul
1780   Hath served a dumb arrest upon his tongue;
Who, mad that sorrow should his use control,
Or keep him from heart-easing words so long,
Begins to talk; but through his lips do throng
1784   Weak words, so thick come in his poor heart's aid
    That no man could distinguish what he said.

Yet sometime 'Tarquin' was pronouncèd plain,
But through his teeth, as if the name he tore.
This windy tempest, till it blow up rain,
Held back his sorrow's tide, to make it more.
At last it rains, and busy winds give o'er;
    Then son and father weep with equal strife
    Who should weep most, for daughter or for wife.

1774 *key-cold* i.e. cold as steel   1775 *pale fear* fearful pallor   1780 *dumb arrest* i.e. injunction of silence   1784 *so thick* so rapidly

The one doth call her his, the other his;
Yet neither may possess the claim they lay.
The father says, 'She's mine.' 'O, mine she is!'
Replies her husband. 'Do not take away
My sorrow's interest. Let no mourner say 1797
 He weeps for her; for she was only mine,
 And only must be wailed by Collatine.'

'O,' quoth Lucretius, 'I did give that life
Which she too early and too late hath spilled.' 1801
'Woe, woe!' quoth Collatine. 'She was my wife,
I owed her, and 'tis mine that she hath killed.' 1803
'My daughter' and 'my wife' with clamors filled
 The dispersed air, who, holding Lucrece' life, 1805
 Answered their cries, 'my daughter' and 'my wife.'

Brutus, who plucked the knife from Lucrece' side,
Seeing such emulation in their woe,
Began to clothe his wit in state and pride, 1809
Burying in Lucrece' wound his folly's show. 1810
He with the Romans was esteemèd so
 As seely jeering idiots are with kings, 1812
 For sportive words and utt'ring foolish things;

But now he throws that shallow habit by 1814
Wherein deep policy did him disguise,
And armed his long-hid wits advisedly
To check the tears in Collatinus' eyes.
'Thou wrongèd lord of Rome,' quoth he, 'arise!
 Let my unsounded self, supposed a fool, 1819
 Now set thy long-experienced wit to school.

1797 *sorrow's interest* claim to sorrow 1801 *late* recently 1803 *owed* owned 1805 *dispersed air* i.e. circumambient air (into which Lucrece's *life* has passed) 1809 *state and pride* i.e. dignified statesmanship 1810 *folly's show* pretense of folly 1812 *seely . . . idiots* i.e. kings' jesters; *seely* simple 1814 *habit* cloak 1819 *unsounded* unplumbed

'Why, Collatine, is woe the cure for woe?
Do wounds help wounds, or grief help grievous deeds?
Is it revenge to give thyself a blow
For his foul act by whom thy fair wife bleeds?
Such childish humor from weak minds proceeds.
   Thy wretched wife mistook the matter so,
    To slay herself that should have slain her foe.

'Courageous Roman, do not steep thy heart
In such relenting dew of lamentations;
But kneel with me, and help to bear thy part
To rouse our Roman gods with invocations
1832   That they will suffer these abominations
     (Since Rome herself in them doth stand disgracèd)
1834   By our strong arms from forth her fair streets chasèd.

'Now, by the Capitol that we adore,
And by this chaste blood so unjustly stainèd,
1837   By heaven's fair sun that breeds the fat earth's store,
By all our country rights in Rome maintainèd,
And by chaste Lucrece' soul that late complainèd
   Her wrongs to us, and by this bloody knife,
    We will revenge the death of this true wife.'

This said, he struck his hand upon his breast
And kissed the fatal knife to end his vow;
1844   And to his protestation urged the rest,
1845   Who, wond'ring at him, did his words allow.
Then jointly to the ground their knees they bow;
   And that deep vow which Brutus made before
    He doth again repeat, and that they swore.

1832 *suffer* allow   1834 *chasèd* i.e. to be chased   1837 *fat* rich, fertile
1844 *to his protestation* i.e. to take a similar vow   1845 *allow* accept

When they had sworn to this advisèd doom,   1849
They did conclude to bear dead Lucrece thence,   1850
To show her bleeding body thorough Rome,
And so to publish Tarquin's foul offense;
Which being done with speedy diligence,
   The Romans plausibly did give consent   1854
   To Tarquin's everlasting banishment.

FINIS

1849 *advisèd doom* deliberate judgment   1850 *to bear* by bearing   1854
plausibly i.e. plausively, with a *general acclamation* (see Argument, line 41)

THE PHOENIX AND
TURTLE

1 Let the bird of loudest lay
2 On the sole Arabian tree
3 Herald sad and trumpet be,
4 To whose sound chaste wings obey,

5 But thou shrieking harbinger,
6 Foul precurrer of the fiend,
7 Augur of the fever's end,
   To this troop come thou not near.

   From this session interdict
10 Every fowl of tyrant wing,
   Save the eagle, feath'red king:
   Keep the obsequy so strict.

   Let the priest in surplice white,
14 That defunctive music can,
15 Be the death-divining swan,
16 Lest the requiem lack his right.

Title: *Phoenix* mythical bird which expires in flame and is reborn in its own ashes, thus symbolizing immortality; *Turtle* turtledove (symbol of true love) 1 *bird . . . lay* i.e. the bird (unidentified) having the loudest song 2 *sole Arabian tree* i.e. the only one of its kind (unidentified) in which the phoenix nests 3 *trumpet* trumpeter 4 *To whose* whose 5 *shrieking harbinger* i.e. the owl 6 *precurrer* precursor 7 *Augur . . . end* i.e. prophet of death 10 *fowl . . . wing* i.e. bird of prey 14 *defunctive music can* i.e. can provide funeral music 15 *death-divining* (in its legendary 'swan-song' occurring only before its death) 16 *his* its

And thou treble-dated crow,   17
That thy sable gender mak'st   18
With the breath thou giv'st and tak'st,   19
'Mongst our mourners shalt thou go.

Here the anthem doth commence:
Love and constancy is dead,
Phoenix and the turtle fled
In a mutual flame from hence.

So they loved as love in twain   25
Had the essence but in one;
Two distincts, division none: 27
Number there in love was slain.   28

Hearts remote, yet not asunder;   29
Distance, and no space was seen
'Twixt this turtle and his queen;
But in them it were a wonder.   32

So between them love did shine
That the turtle saw his right   34
Flaming in the phoenix' sight:
Either was the other's mine.   36

Property was thus appallèd,   37
That the self was not the same;
Single nature's double name   39
Neither two nor one was callèd.

---

17 *treble-dated* i.e. long-lived, the length of three ordinary lives   18 *thy . . . mak'st* i.e. reproduce your own black species   19 *breath* (the crow, or at least the raven, was popularly believed to engender by billing)   25 *So . . . as* i.e. they so loved that   27 *distincts* i.e. distinct persons   28 *slain* i.e. obliterated   29 *remote* i.e. separated in space   32 *But* except (i.e. in them it was simply natural)   34 *right* i.e. due of love   36 *mine* i.e. very own 37–38 *Property . . . same* i.e. the very idea of private possession was thrown into confusion by the obliteration of the distinct or individual possessor 39–40 *Single . . . callèd* i.e. the single nature composed of two persons could be called neither two nor one

41   Reason, in itself confounded,
            Saw division grow together,
            To themselves yet either neither,
44   Simple were so well compounded;

45   That it cried, 'How true a twain
            Seemeth this concordant one!
            Love hath reason, reason none,
48   If what parts can so remain.'

49   Whereupon it made this threne
            To the phoenix and the dove,
            Co-supremes and stars of love,
            As chorus to their tragic scene.

                    THRENOS

            Beauty, truth, and rarity,
            Grace in all simplicity,
55   Here enclosed, in cinders lie.

            Death is now the phoenix' nest;
            And the turtle's loyal breast
            To eternity doth rest,

            Leaving no posterity:
60   'Twas not their infirmity,
61   It was married chastity.

---

41 *in itself confounded* i.e. baffled by its own logical process **44** *Simple* i.e. simples (the individual ingredients in a compound) **45** *it* i.e. Reason **48** *If . . . remain* i.e. if what divides into two can remain one **49** *threne* funeral song (*Threnos*) **55** *Here enclosed* i.e. in the *urn* (cf. line 65) enclosing the *cinders* or ashes **60** *infirmity* i.e. sterility (?) **61** *married chastity* i.e. abstinence in marriage (?)

Truth may seem, but cannot be;   62
Beauty brag, but 'tis not she: 63
Truth and Beauty buried be.

To this urn let those repair
That are either true or fair;
For these dead birds sigh a prayer.

POEMS OF DOUBTFUL
AUTHENTICITY

A Lover's Complaint "By William Shake-speare" was first printed in 1609 in *Shakespeare's Sonnets,* the famous quarto issued by Thomas Thorpe. The poem begins at signature K1ᵛ and concludes the volume. Although critical opinion is divided, it tends, perhaps mistakenly, to deny Shakespeare's authorship of the poem, which is often assigned to some unidentified imitator of Shakespeare, Spenser, Sidney, and Daniel. The present text is based upon the 1609 quarto, and admits only the following material emendations: 7 *sorrow's wind* sorrowes, wind 14 *lattice* lettice 18 *seasoned* seasonèd 68 *aught* ought 80 *Of* O 103 *breathe* breath 112 *manage* mannad'g 118 *Came* Can 208 *the* th' 228 *Hallowed* Hollowèd 241 *Paling* Playing 242 *unconstrainèd* unconstraind 252 *procured* procure 260 *nun* Sunne 265 *stint* sting 284 *flowed* flowèd 293 *O* Or 326 *bestowed* bestowèd 327 *borrowed* borrowèd *owed* owèd 328 *betrayed* betrayèd.

The Passionate Pilgrim "By W. Shakespeare" was printed by William Jaggard in an octavo of 1599. At C3ᵛ, preceding the poem numbered in modern editions XV, the volume has a second title page, *Sonnets to Sundry Notes of Music.* A fragment of another and probably earlier octavo is in the Folger collection, in leaves containing the poems numbered in modern editions I, II, III, IV, V, XVI, XVII, XVIII. Jaggard's volume is an unscrupulously assembled miscellany, containing (a) poems by Shakespeare available elsewhere, (b) poems known to be by writers other than he, and (c) poems of doubtful authorship, some of them reappearing in another miscellany, *England's Helicon,* 1600, or in dubious compilations associated with specific poets.

Omitted from the present edition are the following poems in *The Passionate Pilgrim*, since they are printed from better texts elsewhere in the *Pelican Shakespeare*: I, Sonnet 138; II, Sonnet 144; III, *Love's Labor's Lost*, IV, iii, 55–68; V, *ibid.*, IV, ii, 101–14; XVI, *ibid.*, IV, iii, 96–115. Omitted also is XIX, a version of Marlowe's "The Passionate Shepherd to His Love."

Included are the remaining poems in the miscellany, although some of these can be assigned, with varying degrees of confidence, to particular poets. Numbers IV, VI, IX, and XI are on the Venus and Adonis theme, but they are more likely to have been the work of Bartholomew Griffin than of Shakespeare, Number XI having already appeared in Griffin's *Fidessa*, 1596. Numbers VIII and XX had appeared in Barnfield's *Poems: In Divers Humors*, 1598. Number XII was to reappear in Thomas Deloney's *Garden of Goodwill*, 1631; and Number XVII (as well as XVI, XIX, and, in part, XX) in *England's Helicon*, 1600. Numbers VII, X, XII, XIII, XIV, XV, XVII, XVIII cannot be proved "non-Shakespearean" on the basis of external evidence, but the majority obviously are. Several have merit, but only Number XII is worth the effort to establish a Shakespearean claim.

The present edition is based upon Jaggard's octavo of 1599, with the following material emendations or readings from alternative texts: IV, 5 *ear* eares 10 *figured* figurèd VII, 11 *midst* mids X, 5 *plum* plumbe 8, 9 *left'st* lefts XIII, 9 *with'red* witherèd XIV, 24 *sighed* sight 27 *a moon* an hour XV, 3 *fair'st* fairest XVII, 5 *Love's denying* Love is dying 7 *Heart's renying* Harts nenying 19 *mourn* morn 43 *back* blacke 49 *lass* love 51 *moan* woe XVIII, 4 *fancy (partial) might* fancy (partyall might) 12 *thy* her *sell* sale 14, 17 *ere* yer 45 *be* by 51 *ear* are XX, 22 *beasts* Beares 27–28 (omitted from *The Passionate Pilgrim* and supplied from *England's Helicon*).

A LOVER'S COMPLAINT

1   From off a hill whose concave womb re-worded
2   A plaintful story from a sist'ring vale,
3   My spirits t' attend this double voice accorded,
     And down I laid to list the sad-tuned tale;
5   Ere long espied a fickle maid full pale,
6   Tearing of papers, breaking rings a-twain,
     Storming her world with sorrow's wind and rain.

8   Upon her head a platted hive of straw,
     Which fortified her visage from the sun,
10   Whereon the thought might think sometime it saw
11   The carcass of a beauty spent and done.
12   Time had not scythèd all that youth begun,
13   Nor youth all quit; but, spite of heaven's fell rage,
     Some beauty peeped through lattice of seared age.

1 *womb re-worded* i.e. valley re-echoed 2 *sist'ring* i.e. matching (one similar and nearby) 3 *accorded* inclined 5 *fickle* changeable, perturbed 6 *papers* i.e. love-letters 8 *platted hive* i.e. woven hat 10 *thought* i.e. mind 11 *carcass* remnant 12 *scythèd* cropped, cut down 13 *all quit* i.e. left everything; *fell* deadly

Oft did she heave her napkin to her eyne,   15
Which on it had conceited characters,   16
Laund'ring the silken figures in the brine
That seasoned woe had pelleted in tears,   18
And often reading what contents it bears;
As often shrieking undistinguished woe   20
In clamors of all size, both high and low.

Sometime her levelled eyes their carriage ride,   22
As they did batt'ry to the spheres intend;   23
Sometimes diverted their poor balls are tied
To th' orbèd earth; sometimes they do extend
Their view right on; anon their gazes lend
To every place at once, and, nowhere fixed,
The mind and sight distractedly commixed.

Her hair, nor loose nor tied in formal plat,
Proclaimed in her a careless hand of pride;
For some, untucked, descended her sheaved hat,   31
Hanging her pale and pinèd cheek beside;
Some in her threaden fillet still did bide   33
And, true to bondage, would not break from thence,
Though slackly braided in loose negligence.

---

15 *heave* lift; *napkin* handkerchief   16 *conceited* ingenious   18 *seasoned* (1) matured, (2) salted (punning on *brine*); *pelleted* (1) rounded, (2) prepared as seasoners (punning on 'pellet' as culinary term)   20 *undistinguished* incoherent   22 *levelled* (1) directed, (2) aimed; *carriage ride* move (punning on gun-carriage)   23 *As* as if; *batt'ry . . . spheres* i.e. to direct fire against the heavenly bodies (continuing the artillery metaphor)   31 *sheaved* straw   33 *threaden fillet* i.e. ribbon circling the head

36   A thousand favors from a maund she drew,
37   Of amber, crystal, and of bedded jet,
       Which one by one she in a river threw,
39   Upon whose weeping margent she was set,
       Like usury, applying wet to wet,
       Or monarch's hands that lets not bounty fall
       Where want cries some but where excess begs all.

43   Of folded schedules had she many a one
       Which she perused, sighed, tore, and gave the flood;
45   Cracked many a ring of posied gold and bone,
       Bidding them find their sepulchres in mud;
47   Found yet moe letters sadly penned in blood,
48   With sleided silk feat and affectedly
49   Enswathed and sealed to curious secrecy.

50   These often bathed she in her fluxive eyes,
51   And often kissed, and often gave to tear;
       Cried, 'O false blood, thou register of lies,
53   What unapprovèd witness dost thou bear!
       Ink would have seemed more black and damnèd here!'
       This said, in top of rage the lines she rents,
       Big discontent so breaking their contents.

---

36 *favors* love-tokens; *maund* basket   37 *bedded* inlaid   39 *weeping margent* wet bank   43 *schedules* missives   45 *posied* i.e. inscribed with love-mottoes   47 *moe* more   48 *sleided* ravelled; *feat and affectedly* neatly and lovingly   49 *curious* fastidious   50 *fluxive* flowing   51 *gave* i.e. shared an impulse   53 *unapprovèd* unconfirmed

A reverend man that grazed his cattle nigh,   57
Sometime a blusterer that the ruffle knew   58
Of court, of city, and had let go by   59
The swiftest hours, observèd as they flew,
Towards this afflicted fancy fastly drew,   61
And, privileged by age, desires to know
In brief the grounds and motives of her woe.

So slides he down upon his grainèd bat,   64
And comely-distant sits he by her side ;   65
When he again desires her, being sat,
Her grievance with his hearing to divide :   67
If that from him there may be aught applied
Which may her suffering ecstasy assuage,   69
'Tis promised in the charity of age.

'Father,' she says, 'though in me you behold
The injury of many a blasting hour,
Let it not tell your judgment I am old ;
Not age, but sorrow, over me hath power :
I might as yet have been a spreading flower,
Fresh to myself, if I had self-applied
Love to myself and to no love beside.

---

57 *reverend* aged   58 *ruffle* pretentious bustle   59–60 *had . . . flew* i.e. had gained knowledge through observation during the brief time of youth   61 *fancy* i.e. lady in her love-sick mood; *fastly* closely (?), quickly (?)   64 *grainèd bat* shepherd's staff (so worn as to show the grain)   65 *comely-distant* i.e. at appropriate distance   67 *divide* share   69 *ecstasy* fit

78   'But, woe is me, too early I attended
     A youthful suit – it was to gain my grace –
     Of one by nature's outwards so commended
     That maidens' eyes stuck over all his face :
     Love lacked a dwelling, and made him her place ;
     And when in his fair parts she did abide,
     She was new lodged and newly deified.

     'His browny locks did hang in crooked curls,
86   And every light occasion of the wind
     Upon his lips their silken parcels hurls.
88   What's sweet to do, to do will aptly find :
     Each eye that saw him did enchant the mind,
     For on his visage was in little drawn
91   What largeness thinks in Paradise was sawn.

     'Small show of man was yet upon his chin ;
93   His phoenix down began but to appear,
94   Like unshorn velvet, on that termless skin
95   Whose bare out-bragged the web it seemed to wear.
96   Yet showed his visage by that cost more dear ;
97   And nice affections wavering stood in doubt
     If best were as it was, or best without.

---

78 *attended* gave attention to   86 *occasion* occurrence, i.e. movement   88
What's . . . find i.e. what's pleasant to do is readily done   91 *largeness* i.e.
in large (in opposition to *in little*); *thinks* i.e. one thinks; *sawn* seen   93
phoenix down i.e. incipient beard signalling the inevitable birth of man
from boy (?)   94 *termless* i.e. young   95 *out-bragged* out-braved   96 *by
that cost* i.e. by that expense, for that very reason   97 *nice affections* fastidious taste

'His qualities were beauteous as his form,
For maiden-tongued he was, and thereof free;   100
Yet, if men moved him, was he such a storm
As oft 'twixt May and April is to see,
When winds breathe sweet, unruly though they be.
His rudeness so with his authorized youth   104
Did livery falseness in a pride of truth.   105

'Well could he ride, and often men would say,
"That horse his mettle from his rider takes.
Proud of subjection, noble by the sway,
What rounds, what bounds, what course, what stop he
    makes!"
And controversy hence a question takes,   110
Whether the horse by him became his deed,   111
Or he his manage by th' well-doing steed.   112

'But quickly on this side the verdict went: 113
His real habitude gave life and grace   114
To appertainings and to ornament,   115
Accomplished in himself, not in his case.   116
All aids, themselves made fairer by their place,
Came for additions; yet their purposed trim   118
Pieced not his grace but were all graced by him. 119

100 *maiden-tongued* modest-spoken; *free* innocent   104 *His rudeness so* his
turbulent behavior then; *authorized* privileged   105 *livery falseness* i.e.
cloak or conceal indecorousness; *truth* decorum   110 *takes* takes up, becomes involved in   111 *by . . . deed* i.e. was exalted because of him   112
his . . . steed i.e. excelled in horsemanship because of the skill of the steed
113 *this* i.e. the following   114 *real habitude* i.e. inborn characteristics
115 *appertainings* things associated with him   116 *case* outsides   118 *Came
for additions* came in for advantages; *yet . . . trim* i.e. always their intended
improvement   119 *Pieced* mended

'So on the tip of his subduing tongue
All kinds of arguments and question deep,
122 All replication prompt and reason strong,
123 For his advantage still did wake and sleep.
To make the weeper laugh, the laugher weep,
125 He had the dialect and different skill,
126 Catching all passions in his craft of will;

127 'That he did in the general bosom reign
128 Of young, of old, and sexes both enchanted
To dwell with him in thoughts, or to remain
130 In personal duty, following where he haunted.
Consents bewitched, ere he desire, have granted,
132 And dialogued for him what he would say,
133 Asked their own wills and made their wills obey.

'Many there were that did his picture get,
135 To serve their eyes, and in it put their mind;
Like fools that in th' imagination set
The goodly objects which abroad they find
Of lands and mansions, theirs in thought assigned,
139 And laboring in moe pleasures to bestow them
140 Than the true gouty landlord which doth owe them.

---

122 *replication prompt* quick rejoinders   123 *wake and sleep* i.e. flow and ebb   125 *dialect* discourse; *different* varying   126 *craft of will* power of persuasion   127 *That* so that   128 *enchanted* charmed, i.e. influenced   130 *haunted* frequented   132 *dialogued . . . say* spoke his part as well as their own   133 *Asked* made demands upon   135 *put their mind* i.e. used their imaginations   139 *laboring . . . them* i.e. laboring to extract more pleasure from them   140 *gouty* rheumatic, i.e. old; *owe* own

'So many have, that never touched his hand,
Sweetly supposed them mistress of his heart.
My woeful self, that did in freedom stand
And was my own fee-simple, not in part,   144
What with his art in youth and youth in art,
Threw my affections in his charmèd power,
Reserved the stalk and gave him all my flower.

'Yet did I not, as some my equals did,   148
Demand of him, nor being desirèd yielded.   149
Finding myself in honor so forbid,
With safest distance I mine honor shielded.
Experience for me many bulwarks builded   152
Of proofs new-bleeding, which remained the foil   153
Of this false jewel, and his amorous spoil.

'But, ah, who ever shunned by precedent
The destined ill she must herself assay?
Or forced examples, 'gainst her own content,   157
To put the by-past perils in her way?   158
Counsel may stop awhile what will not stay;   159
For when we rage, advice is often seen   160
By blunting us to make our wits more keen.   161

---

144 *my . . . part* i.e. wholly, not partly, at my own disposal (like land in
freehold) 148 *my equals* i.e. those like me, my kind 149 *Demand . . .
yielded* i.e. yield to my own desires or his 152 *Experience* knowledge,
awareness; *bulwarks* i.e. restraints 153 *proofs new-bleeding* i.e. persons
recently victimized; *foil* i.e. dark ground against which he shone 157 *forced*
gave weight to; *content* presumed satisfaction 158 *To . . . way* i.e. to raise as
obstacles the past perils (of others) 159 *stop awhile* i.e. only check 160
rage i.e. are aroused 161 *By . . . keen* i.e. to sharpen our wits by opposition
(with *blunting us* used in a forced antithesis)

162   'Nor gives it satisfaction to our blood
163   That we must curb it upon others' proof,
164   To be forbod the sweets that seems so good
165   For fear of harms that preach in our behoof.
166   O appetite, from judgment stand aloof!
        The one a palate hath that needs will taste,
        Though Reason weep and cry, "It is thy last."

169   'For further I could say this man's untrue,
        And knew the patterns of his foul beguiling;
171   Heard where his plants in others' orchards grew;
        Saw how deceits were gilded in his smiling;
173   Knew vows were ever brokers to defiling;
174   Thought characters and words merely but art,
175   And bastards of his foul adulterate heart.

176   'And long upon these terms I held my city,
        Till thus he 'gan besiege me: "Gentle maid,
        Have of my suffering youth some feeling pity
        And be not of my holy vows afraid.
180   That's to ye sworn to none was ever said;
181   For feasts of love I have been called unto,
        Till now did ne'er invite nor never woo.

---

162 *blood* passion   163 *proof* example   164 *forbod* forbidden   165 *harms* . . . *behoof* i.e. dangers which give good counsel   166 *stand aloof* i.e. remain ever unreconciled   169 *say* . . . *untrue* i.e. tell of this man's untruth   171 *plants* i.e. adulterate offspring; *orchards* gardens   173 *brokers* panders   174 *characters and words* i.e. written and spoken words   175 *bastards* i.e. base offspring   176 *city* i.e. citadel of chastity   180 *That's* what's   181 *called unto* invited, solicited

' "All my offenses that abroad you see
Are errors of the blood, none of the mind.
Love made them not. With acture they may be,   185
Where neither party is nor true nor kind.
They sought their shame that so their shame did find;
And so much less of shame in me remains
By how much of me their reproach contains.   189

' "Among the many that mine eyes have seen,
Not one whose flame my heart so much as warmèd,
Or my affection put to th' smallest teen,   192
Or any of my leisures ever charmèd.
Harm have I done to them, but ne'er was harmèd;
Kept hearts in liveries, but mine own was free   195
And reigned commanding in his monarchy.

' "Look here what tributes wounded fancies sent me
Of pallid pearls and rubies red as blood,
Figuring that they their passions likewise lent me
Of grief and blushes, aptly understood
In bloodless white and the encrimsoned mood –   201
Effects of terror and dear modesty,
Encamped in hearts, but fighting outwardly.

---

185 *acture* i.e. mechanical action   189 *By . . . contains* i.e. the more they
reproach me   192 *teen* stress   195 *liveries* garments of service   201 *mood*
mode

204   ' "And, lo, behold these talents of their hair,
205   With twisted metal amorously empleached,
206   I have received from many a several fair,
         Their kind acceptance weepingly beseeched,
208   With the annexions of fair gems enriched,
209   And deep-brained sonnets that did amplify
         Each stone's dear nature, worth, and quality.

         ' "The diamond – why, 'twas beautiful and hard,
212   Whereto his invised properties did tend;
213   The deep-green em'rald, in whose fresh regard
214   Weak sights their sickly radiance do amend;
215   The heaven-hued sapphire, and the opal blend
         With objects manifold : each several stone,
217   With wit well blazoned, smiled or made some moan.

218   ' "Lo, all these trophies of affections hot,
219   Of pensived and subdued desires the tender,
         Nature hath charged me that I hoard them not,
         But yield them up where I myself must render :
222   That is, to you, my origin and ender;
         For these of force must your oblations be,
224   Since I their altar, you enpatron me.

---

204 *talents* i.e. golden riches   205 *empleached* entwined   206 *many . . . fair* many different fair ones   208 *annexions* additions (to the gold settings of the locks of hair)   209 *deep-brained* learned; *amplify* expatiate upon 212 *his invised* i.e. seen within it (?)   213 *regard* aspect   214 *radiance* power of vision   215–16 *blend . . . manifold* with the blended colors of many objects (?)   217 *blazoned* proclaimed (in the accompanying sonnets) 218 *affections* passions   219 *pensived* saddened; *tender* offering   222 *my . . . ender* i.e. my beginning and end, my all   224 *Since . . . enpatron me* i.e. since you are the patron or founder of me (the altar at which they are offered)

'"O, then, advance of yours that phraseless hand   225
Whose white weighs down the airy scale of praise!
Take all these similes to your own command,   227
Hallowed with sighs that burning lungs did raise.
What me, your minister, for you obeys,   229
Works under you; and to your audit comes   230
Their distract parcels in combinèd sums.   231

'"Lo, this device was sent me from a nun,
Or sister sanctified, of holiest note,
Which late her noble suit in court did shun,   234
Whose rarest havings made the blossoms dote;   235
For she was sought by spirits of richest coat,   236
But kept cold distance, and did thence remove
To spend her living in eternal love.   238

'"But, O my sweet, what labor is't to leave   239
The thing we have not, mast'ring what not strives,
Paling the place which did no form receive,   241
Playing patient sports in unconstrainèd gyves?   242
She that her fame so to herself contrives,   243
The scars of battle 'scapeth by the flight   244
And makes her absence valiant, not her might.   245

---

225 *phraseless* indescribable   227 *similes* love-tokens and accompanying sonnets   229 *What . . . obeys* i.e. whatever pays homage to me as minister to you   230 *audit* accounting   231 *distract* separate   234 *suit* attendance   235 *havings* personal gifts; *blossoms* i.e. flower of the nobility   236 *coat* i.e. heraldry, descent   238 *eternal love* i.e. love of the divine   239 *leave* i.e. renounce (ironic comment upon nun retreating from love which she did not feel)   241 *Paling . . . receive* i.e. fencing an undefined area   242 *Playing . . . gyves* i.e. pretending patiently to endure bonds which do not exist   243 *her . . . contrives* i.e. creates for herself the reputation for renouncing love   244 *scars . . . flight* i.e. avoids the wounds of a true encounter   245 *her absence* i.e. fictitious reputation because of absence; *might* true power (to resist love)

'"O, pardon me, in that my boast is true:
The accident which brought me to her eye
Upon the moment did her force subdue,
And now she would the cagèd cloister fly.
250 Religious love put out religion's eye.
251 Not to be tempted, would she be inured,
252 And now, to tempt all, liberty procured.

'"How mighty then you are, O hear me tell:
254 The broken bosoms that to me belong
Have emptied all their fountains in my well,
And mine I pour your ocean all among.
257 I strong o'er them, and you o'er me being strong,
258 Must for your victory us all congest,
259 As compound love to physic your cold breast.

'"My parts had pow'r to charm a sacred nun,
Who, disciplined, ay, dieted in grace,
262 Believed her eyes when they t' assail begun,
All vows and consecrations giving place.
264 O most potential love! vow, bond, nor space
265 In thee hath neither stint, knot, nor confine,
For thou art all, and all things else are thine.

---

250 *Religious . . . eye* i.e. worshipful love (of the speaker) cancelled her love of the divine **251** *inured* steeled **252** *tempt* venture **254** *bosoms* i.e. hearts **257** *strong* victorious **258** *congest* gather together **259** *physic . . . breast* i.e. cure the existing 'congestion' **262** *Believed . . . begun* i.e. put her faith in her eyes when assailed by what they saw **264** *space* i.e. place (of confinement) **265** *knot* binding force

'"When thou impressest, what are precepts worth   267
Of stale example? When thou wilt inflame,
How coldly those impediments stand forth   269
Of wealth, of filial fear, law, kindred, fame!
Love's arms are peace, 'gainst rule, 'gainst sense,   271
   'gainst shame;
And sweetens, in the suff'ring pangs it bears,
The aloes of all forces, shocks, and fears.   273

'"Now all these hearts that do on mine depend,
Feeling it break, with bleeding groans they pine;
And supplicant their sighs to you extend,   276
To leave the batt'ry that you make 'gainst mine,
Lending soft audience to my sweet design,
And credent soul to that strong-bonded oath   279
That shall prefer and undertake my troth."   280

'This said, his wat'ry eyes he did dismount,   281
Whose sights till then were levelled on my face;
Each cheek a river running from a fount
With brinish current downward flowed apace.
O, how the channel to the stream gave grace!
Who glazed with crystal gate the glowing roses   286
That flame through water which their hue encloses.

267 *impressest* conscript   269 *stand forth* appear   271 *are peace* effect
victory   273 *aloes* i.e. bitters   276 *supplicant* i.e. as supplicant   279 *credent*
believing, trusting   280 *prefer* advance; *undertake* support   281 *dismount*
lower   286 *Who* which

'O father, what a hell of witchcraft lies
In the small orb of one particular tear!
But with the inundation of the eyes
What rocky heart to water will not wear!
What breast so cold that is not warmèd here,
293   O cleft effect! cold modesty, hot wrath,
294   Both fire from hence and chill extincture hath.

'For, lo, his passion, but an art of craft,
296   Even there resolved my reason into tears;
297   There my white stole of chastity I daffed,
Shook off my sober guards and civil fears;
299   Appear to him as he to me appears,
300   All melting; though our drops this diff'rence bore:
His poisoned me, and mine did him restore.

'In him a plenitude of subtle matter,
303   Applied to cautels, all strange forms receives,
Of burning blushes, or of weeping water,
305   Or sounding paleness; and he takes and leaves,
306   In either's aptness, as it best deceives,
To blush at speeches rank, to weep at woes,
308   Or to turn white and sound at tragic shows;

---

293 *cleft* divided, double   294 *extincture* extinguishing   296 *resolved* dissolved   297 *daffed* doffed   299 *Appear* I appear   300 *drops* medicinal drops   303 *cautels* trickeries, deceits   305 *sounding* swooning; *takes and leaves* i.e. alternately employs   306 *In . . . aptness* i.e. each thing's immediate usefulness   308 *sound* swoon

'That not a heart which in his level came 309
Could 'scape the hail of his all-hurting aim, 310
Showing fair nature is both kind and tame; 311
And, veiled in them, did win whom he would maim. 312
Against the thing he sought he would exclaim:
When he most burned in heart-wished luxury, 314
He preached pure maid and praised cold chastity.

'Thus merely with the garment of a Grace
The naked and concealèd fiend he covered;
That th' unexperient gave the tempter place, 318
Which, like a cherubin, above them hovered. 319
Who, young and simple, would not be so lovered?
Ay me! I fell, and yet do question make
What I should do again for such a sake.

'O, that infected moisture of his eye, 323
O, that false fire which in his cheek so glowed,
O, that forced thunder from his heart did fly,
O, that sad breath his spongy lungs bestowed, 326
O, all that borrowed motion seeming owed, 327
Would yet again betray the fore-betrayed
And new pervert a reconcilèd maid!' 329

FINIS

309 *level* i.e. sights 310 *hail* i.e. bullets 311 *Showing . . . is* i.e. appearing
to be in his nature 312 *them* i.e. kindness and tameness 314 *luxury*
lechery 318 *th' unexperient . . . place* i.e. the inexperienced admitted the
tempter 319 *Which . . . cherubin* i.e. who, like an angel 323 *infected* infec-
tious 326 *spongy* i.e. diseased 327 *borrowed . . . owed* i.e. assumed
behavior seemingly his own 329 *reconcilèd* penitent

IV

1 Sweet Cytherea, sitting by a brook
2 With young Adonis, lovely, fresh, and green,
3 Did court the lad with many a lovely look,
Such looks as none could look but beauty's queen.
She told him stories to delight his ear;
6 She showed him favors to allure his eye;
To win his heart she touched him here and there —
Touches so soft still conquer chastity.
9 But whether unripe years did want conceit,
10 Or he refused to take her figured proffer,
The tender nibbler would not touch the bait,
But smile and jest at every gentle offer.
13   Then fell she on her back, fair queen, and toward.
14   He rose and ran away. Ah, fool too froward!

VI

Scarce had the sun dried up the dewy morn,
And scarce the herd gone to the hedge for shade,
When Cytherea, all in love forlorn,
4 A longing tarriance for Adonis made
5 Under an osier growing by a brook,
6 A brook where Adon used to cool his spleen.

IV   1 *Cytherea* Venus   2 *green* i.e. new-grown   3 *lovely* loving   6 *favors*
charms, gracious appearances   9 *conceit* understanding   10 *figured* sig-
nalled   13 *toward* tractable, willing   14 *froward* recalcitrant
VI   4 *tarriance* period of waiting   5 *osier* willow   6 *spleen* heat

Hot was the day; she hotter that did look
For his approach that often there had been.
Anon he comes, and throws his mantle by, 9
And stood stark naked on the brook's green brim.
The sun looked on the world with glorious eye,
Yet not so wistly as this queen on him. 12
 He, spying her, bounced in whereas he stood. 13
 'O Jove,' quoth she, 'why was not I a flood!'

VII

Fair is my love, but not so fair as fickle;
Mild as a dove, but neither true nor trusty;
Brighter than glass, and yet as glass is, brittle;
Softer than wax, and yet as iron rusty:
 A lily pale, with damask dye, to grace her; 5
 None fairer, nor none falser, to deface her. 6

Her lips to mine how often hath she joinèd,
Between each kiss her oaths of true love swearing!
How many tales to please me hath she coinèd,
Dreading my love, the loss whereof still fearing! 9
 Yet, in the midst of all her pure protestings,
 Her faith, her oaths, her tears, and all were jestings.

She burnt with love, as straw with fire flameth;
She burnt out love, as soon as straw outburneth;
She framed the love, and yet she foiled the framing; 15
She bade love last, and yet she fell a-turning. 16
 Was this a lover, or a lecher whether? 17
 Bad in the best, though excellent in neither.

9 *Anon* presently 12 *wistly* eagerly 13 *whereas* whereat
VII 5 *damask* mingled red and white (of the damask rose); *to . . . her* i.e.
to her credit 6 *to deface her* i.e. to her discredit 9 *coinèd* counterfeited
15 *framed* formed, created; *foiled* countered 16 *fell a-turning* i.e. proved
fickle 17 *whether* i.e. which of the two

VIII

If music and sweet poetry agree,
As they must needs (the sister and the brother),
Then must the love be great 'twixt thee and me,
Because thou lov'st the one, and I the other.
5   Dowland to thee is dear, whose heavenly touch
Upon the lute doth ravish human sense;
7   Spenser to me, whose deep conceit is such
8   As, passing all conceit, needs no defense.
Thou lov'st to hear the sweet melodious sound
10   That Phoebus' lute (the queen of music) makes;
And I in deep delight am chiefly drowned
When as himself to singing he betakes.
13   One god is god of both, as poets feign;
14   One knight loves both, and both in thee remain.

IX

Fair was the morn when the fair queen of love,
2   *   *   *   *   *   *   *
Paler for sorrow than her milk-white dove,
For Adon's sake, a youngster proud and wild,
5   Her stand she takes upon a steep-up hill.
Anon Adonis comes with horn and hounds.
She, silly queen, with more than love's good will,
Forbade the boy he should not pass those grounds.
'Once,' quoth she, 'did I see a fair sweet youth
Here in these brakes deep-wounded with a boar,
11   Deep in the thigh, a spectacle of ruth!
See, in my thigh,' quoth she, 'here was the sore.'

VIII 5 *Dowland* John Dowland, lutenist and composer 7 *Spenser* Edmund Spenser, author of *The Faerie Queene*; *deep conceit* resourceful creativeness 8 *passing all conceit* surpassing all imagination 10 *Phoebus* Apollo, musician of the gods 13 *feign* i.e. say in their creations 14 *One knight* (conjectured to be Sir George Carey, to whom was dedicated Dowland's first book of airs, 1597, and to whose wife was dedicated Spenser's *Muiopotmos*, 1590)

IX 2 (the line rhyming with *wild* is missing) 5 *steep-up* sharply rising 11 *ruth* pity

She showèd hers ; he saw more wounds than one,
And blushing fled and left her all alone.

X

Sweet rose, fair flower, untimely plucked, soon vaded,   1
Plucked in the bud, and vaded in the spring !
Bright orient pearl, alack, too timely shaded !   3
Fair creature, killed too soon by death's sharp sting !
    Like a green plum that hangs upon a tree,
    And falls, through wind, before the fall should be.

I weep for thee, and yet no cause I have ;
For why, thou left'st me nothing in thy will :   8
And yet thou left'st me more than I did crave ;
For why, I cravèd nothing of thee still.
    O yes, dear friend, I pardon crave of thee :
    Thy discontent thou didst bequeath to me.

XI

Venus, with young Adonis sitting by her
Under a myrtle shade, began to woo him.
She told the youngling how god Mars did try her,   3
And as he fell to her, she fell to him.   4
'Even thus,' quoth she, 'the warlike god embraced me,'
And then she clipped Adonis in her arms.
'Even thus,' quoth she, 'the warlike god unlaced me,'   7
As if the boy should use like loving charms.
'Even thus,' quoth she, 'he seizèd on my lips,'
And with her lips on his did act the seizure ;
And as she fetchèd breath, away he skips,
And would not take her meaning nor her pleasure.   12
    Ah, that I had my lady at this bay,   13
    To kiss and clip me till I run away !   14

X   1 *vaded* faded   3 *timely* soon   8 *For why* because
XI   3 *try* attempt   4 *he . . . her* i.e. he fell to her lot (with ribald pun on second *fell*   7 *unlaced* i.e. undressed   12 *pleasure* proffered gratification
13 *bay* stand   14 *clip* embrace

XII

Crabbed age and youth cannot live together:
2   Youth is full of pleasance, age is full of care;
Youth like summer morn, age like winter weather;
Youth like summer brave, age like winter bare.
Youth is full of sport, age's breath is short;
Youth is nimble, age is lame;
Youth is hot and bold, age is weak and cold;
Youth is wild, and age is tame.
Age, I do abhor thee; youth, I do adore thee.
O, my love, my love is young!
11   Age, I do defy thee. O sweet shepherd, hie thee,
12   For methinks thou stays too long.

XIII

Beauty is but a vain and doubtful good;
2   A shining gloss that vadeth suddenly;
A flower that dies when first it 'gins to bud;
4   A brittle glass that's broken presently;
    A doubtful good, a gloss, a glass, a flower,
    Lost, vaded, broken, dead within an hour.

7   And as goods lost are seld or never found,
As vaded gloss no rubbing will refresh,
As flowers dead lie with'red on the ground,
10   As broken glass no cement can redress:
    So beauty blemished once, for ever lost,
12   In spite of physic, painting, pain, and cost.

XII   **2** *pleasance* cheer   **11** *hie thee* hasten   **12** *stays* delayest
XIII   **2** *vadeth* fades   **4** *presently* at once   **7** *seld* seldom   **10** *redress*
repair   **12** *physic* medicine; *cost* expenditures

XIV

Good night, good rest. Ah, neither be my share!
She bade good night that kept my rest away,
And daffed me to a cabin hanged with care   3
To descant on the doubts of my decay.   4
   'Farewell,' quoth she, 'and come again to-morrow.'
   Fare well I could not, for I supped with sorrow.

Yet at my parting sweetly did she smile,
In scorn or friendship, nill I conster whether.   8
'T may be she joyed to jest at my exile;
'T may be, again to make me wander thither:
   'Wander' – a word for shadows like myself
   As take the pain but cannot pluck the pelf.   12

Lord, how mine eyes throw gazes to the east!
My heart doth charge the watch; the morning rise   14
Doth cite each moving sense from idle rest,   15
Not daring trust the office of mine eyes,
   While Philomela sits and sings, I sit and mark,   17
   And wish her lays were tunèd like the lark;   18

For she doth welcome daylight with her ditty
And drives away dark dreaming night.
The night so packed, I post unto my pretty;   21
Heart hath his hope, and eyes their wishèd sight;
   Sorrow changed to solace and solace mixed with sorrow;
   For why, she sighed and bade me come to-morrow.

XIV   3 *daffed* doffed, sent off; *hanged* furnished   4 *descant* enlarge, expatiate; *doubts* fears   8 *nill . . . whether* I know not which   12 *pelf* reward, booty   14 *charge* i.e. keep watch over   15 *cite* incite   17 *Philomela* the nightingale   18 *tunèd . . . lark* i.e. attuned to the morn   21 *packed* disposed of

25 Were I with her, the night would post too soon,
26 But now are minutes added to the hours;
27 To spite me now, each minute seems a moon;
    Yet not for me, shine sun to succor flowers!
      Pack night, peep day! Good day, of night now borrow:
30   Short, night, to-night, and length thyself to-morrow.

XV

1 It was a lording's daughter, the fairest one of three,
2 That likèd of her master as well as well might be,
    Till looking on an Englishman, the fair'st that eye could see,
      Her fancy fell a-turning.
    Long was the combat doubtful that love with love did fight,
    To leave the master loveless, or kill the gallant knight:
7 To put in practice either, alas, it was a spite
      Unto the silly damsel!
9 But one must be refusèd; more mickle was the pain
    That nothing could be usèd to turn them both to gain,
    For of the two the trusty knight was wounded with disdain:
      Alas, she could not help it!
13 Thus art with arms contending was victor of the day,
    Which by a gift of learning did bear the maid away:
15 Then, lullaby, the learned man hath got the lady gay;
      For now my song is ended.

XVII

    My flocks feed not,
    My ewes breed not,
    My rams speed not,
      All is amiss:

---

25 *post* hasten on   26 *added to* i.e. made to resemble   27 *moon* month   30 *Short . . . length* shorten . . . lengthen

XV   1 *lording's* lord's   2 *master* teacher, tutor   7 *put in practice* i.e. act upon, come to a decision about   9 *mickle* great   13 *art* learning   15 *lullaby* good night

Love's denying,
Faith's defying,   6
Heart's renying,   7
   Causer of this.
All my merry jigs are quite forgot,
All my lady's love is lost, God wot.
Where her faith was firmly fixed in love,
There a nay is placed without remove.
One silly cross   13
Wrought all my loss.
   O frowning Fortune, cursèd fickle dame!
For now I see
Inconstancy
   More in women than in men remain.

In black mourn I,
All fears scorn I,
Love hath forlorn me,   21
   Living in thrall.
Heart is bleeding,
All help needing –
O cruel speeding,   25
   Fraughted with gall!   26
My shepherd's pipe can sound no deal;   27
My wether's bell rings doleful knell;
My curtail dog, that wont to have played,   29
Plays not at all, but seems afraid;
With sighs so deep
Procures to weep,
   In howling wise, to see my doleful plight.
How sighs resound
Through heartless ground,   35
   Like a thousand vanquished men in bloody fight!

XVII 6 *defying* rejection 7 *renying* forswearing, disowning 13 *cross* misfortune 21 *forlorn me* rendered me forlorn 25 *speeding* progress, journey 26 *Fraughted* laden 27 *no deal* not at all 29 *curtail* dock-tailed 35 *heartless* desolate (?), pitiless (?)

Clear wells spring not,
Sweet birds sing not,
Green plants bring not
Forth their dye.
Herds stand weeping,
Flocks all sleeping,
Nymphs back peeping
   Fearfully.
All our pleasure known to us poor swains,
All our merry meetings on the plains,
All our evening sport from us is fled,
All our love is lost, for love is dead.
Farewell, sweet lass!
Thy like ne'er was
   For a sweet content, the cause of all my moan.
Poor Corydon
Must live alone.
   Other help for him I see that there is none.

XVIII

When as thine eye hath chose the dame
2   And stalled the deer that thou shouldst strike,
Let reason rule things worthy blame,
4   As well as fancy (partial) might;
   Take counsel of some wiser head,
   Neither too young, nor yet unwed.

And when thou com'st thy tale to tell,
8   Smooth not thy tongue with filèd talk,
9   Lest she some subtile practice smell—
10   A cripple soon can find a halt;

XVIII **2** *stalled* brought to a stand   **4** *fancy (partial) might* (so punctuated the words suggest that 'partial' affection should share rule with impartial reason; but the passage remains obscure)   **8** *filèd* polished   **9** *practice* plot   **10** *A cripple . . . halt* (proverb resembling 'Set a thief to catch a thief'); *halt* limp

178

But plainly say thou lov'st her well,
And set thy person forth to sell.

What though her frowning brows be bent,
Her cloudy looks will calm ere night;
And then too late she will repent
That thus dissembled her delight,
    And twice desire, ere it be day,
    That which with scorn she put away.

What though she strive to try her strength,
And ban and brawl and say thee nay,   20
Her feeble force will yield at length,
When craft hath taught her thus to say:
    'Had women been so strong as men,
    In faith, you had not had it then.'

And to her will frame all thy ways.
Spare not to spend, and chiefly there
Where thy desert may merit praise
By ringing in thy lady's ear.
    The strongest castle, tower, and town,
    The golden bullet beats it down.

Serve always with assurèd trust
And in thy suit be humble-true.
Unless thy lady prove unjust,   33
Press never thou to choose a new.
    When time shall serve, be thou not slack
    To proffer, though she put thee back.

The wiles and guiles that women work,
Dissembled with an outward show,
The tricks and toys that in them lurk,
The cock that treads them shall not know.
    Have you not heard it said full oft,
    A woman's nay doth stand for naught?

20 *ban* curse   **33** *unjust* untrue, faithless

43   Think women still to strive with men
44   To sin, and never for to saint.
45   There is no heaven : be holy then
             When time with age shall them attaint.
               Were kisses all the joys in bed,
               One woman would another wed.

             But soft, enough ! too much, I fear ;
             Lest that my mistress hear my song.
51   She will not stick to round me on th' ear,
             To teach my tongue to be so long.
               Yet will she blush, here be it said,
54   To hear her secrets so bewrayed.

XX

             As it fell upon a day
             In the merry month of May,
             Sitting in a pleasant shade
             Which a grove of myrtles made,
             Beasts did leap and birds did sing,
             Trees did grow and plants did spring ;
             Everything did banish moan,
             Save the nightingale alone.
             She, poor bird, as all forlorn,
10   Leaned her breast up-till a thorn
             And there sung the dolefull'st ditty,
             That to hear it was great pity.
             'Fie, fie, fie !' now would she cry ;
             'Tereu, tereu !' by and by ;
             That to hear her so complain
             Scarce I could from tears refrain ;
             For her griefs, so lively shown,
             Made me think upon mine own.

43 *Think* believe   44 *to saint* i.e. to be saintly   45 *There* i.e. in women   51 *stick . . . ear* i.e. hesitate to scold   54 *bewrayed* revealed

'Ah,' thought I, 'thou mourn'st in vain;
None takes pity on thy pain.
Senseless trees they cannot hear thee;
Ruthless beasts they will not cheer thee.
King Pandion, he is dead;   23
All thy friends are lapped in lead;
All thy fellow birds do sing,
Careless of thy sorrowing.
[Even so, poor bird, like thee,
None alive will pity me.]
Whilst as fickle Fortune smiled,
Thou and I were both beguiled.'
Every one that flatters thee
Is no friend in misery.
Words are easy, like the wind;
Faithful friends are hard to find.
Every man will be thy friend
Whilst thou hast wherewith to spend;
But if store of crowns be scant,
No man will supply thy want.
If that one be prodigal,
Bountiful they will him call,
And with such-like flattering,
'Pity but he were a king.'   42
If he be addict to vice,
Quickly him they will entice.
If to women he be bent,
They have at commandement.
But if fortune once do frown,
Then farewell his great renown!
They that fawned on him before
Use his company no more.
He that is thy friend indeed,
He will help thee in thy need.

xx 23 *Pandion* a king of Athens, father of the ravished Philomela, who
was transformed into the nightingale; cf. Ovid, *Metamorphoses*, VI, 424–676
42 *but he* that he was not

If thou sorrow, he will weep;
If thou wake, he cannot sleep.
Thus of every grief in heart
He with thee doth bear a part.
These are certain signs to know
Faithful friend from flatt'ring foe.

For a complete list of books available from Penguin in the United States, write to Dept. DG, Penguin Books, 299 Murray Hill Parkway, East Rutherford, New Jersey 07073.

For a complete list of books available from Penguin in Canada, write to Penguin Books Canada Limited, 2801 John Street, Markham, Ontario L3R 1B4.

If you live in the British Isles, write to Dept. EP, Penguin Books Ltd, Harmondsworth, Middlesex.